THE PSI WARS

LASZLO GUBANYI

Published by LASZLO GUBANYI, 2023.

THE PSI WARS

First edition. June 25, 2023.

Written by LASZLO GUBANYI.

CHAPTER ONE

"Hello bunny!"

The deep, raspy voice sounded unnatural coming from the little blond girl sitting on the grass.

The rabbit curiously approached her, sniffed her knees, then crouched down next to her, putting its head on her thigh.

"Good bunny. You too are alone. Don't worry, we'll be alright together."

They were quiet for a while. The rabbit closed its eyes and appeared to be asleep whilst the girl just sat and watched the yellow flowers in front of her. She found the bees buzzing around from flower to flower fascinating.

"Hello bees, you are early today."

She extended her hand and the bees rested on her fingers.

"Hello bees, this is bunny, my new friend. We were very lonely, but now we are happy, together."

The rabbit didn't bother to open its eyes.

The bees were buzzing on her fingers.

There was a peaceful quietness in the air.......

The peace was suddenly interrupted by the call from her mother.

Sarah!

Both the rabbit and the bees disappeared much to Sarah's disappointment.

She liked animals. She could communicate with them. Not like the people around her who just made a lot of noise with their mouths, something that Sarah found very hard to understand. Why couldn't people be just simple, and nice, like animals?

Sarah lifted her face to that yellow heat from above.

It felt nice on her face. She welcomed its warmth. She could feel her face absorbing that heat which then travelled down, filling her chest with light.

It felt good.

Sarah knew her face was different.

She knew that she was different.

She had a lot of knowledge inside her, but could not understand the world around.

Especially people.

Animals were OK.

Even trees and flowers were okay.

She could understand the river, the wind.

She could not understand people and people could not understand her.

For them she was born nearly sixteen years ago and had the intellect of a six year old.

Her mother was told by the doctors that she had Down's Syndrome, which, though was a nice name, did not really explain why she was stuck with a child like Sarah.

Not that there were any problems with the girl.

She was a very quiet and loving child, always seeking hugs from her mother.

She was always doing what she was told to do, providing she understood what she was supposed to do.

She was no trouble at all.

All her mother had to do was to take her to any place where there was grass, trees and flowers, sit her down, and many hours later she would find her sitting on the same spot watching the flowers with a smile on her face, perfectly happy in her own world.

She avoided people and other children as they were usually mean to her.

Animals were not like that.

They came to see her, accepting her company.

Even the trees seemed to bend down, stroking her hair with their leaves.

The sunlight, the wind, everything was nice to her.

No one appeared to notice, but it never rained when she was **out**.At night, though, it was different.

There were no visits from animals .

There were mice for a while but her mother got rid of them.

She was alone and she was afraid.

The cracks and creaks of the old house frightened her.

The shadows had very unfriendly shapes at night.

Many a night she would seek refuge in her mother's bed, cuddled up to her for protection.

For some reason, on these nights, her mother slept much better.

Sarah's mother, Therezia, was a simple, hard working woman. She spent her days washing and ironing other people's clothing to keep a roof over their heads, something that was not an easy task on her own, but there was no one to help her.

Therezia became pregnant when she was about eighteen years old and she had no idea that she was pregnant.

The first time she knew there was something not quite right was when she noticed her mother looking at her stomach suspiciously.

Then the pregnancy was confirmed and she found that she had a lot of explaining to do.

Except – there was nothing she could actually explain.

She was not completely naive, she knew how one would get pregnant, but she insisted that she had never been with a man.

She was not raped, obviously she would remember that.

Her mother naturally was quite upset about the pregnancy.
She insisted on being told what happened.
She took her to a psychiatrist who after a few sessions
decided that Therezia must have had a very traumatic
experience and was trying to protect her sanity by denying the
incident.
His advice to the mother was just to let her deal with the
problem in her own way.
Her mother was not very happy about this but there was
nothing else she could do.
The fact remained; Therezia was pregnant, but it really did not
seem to affect her at all.
She was quite happy about being pregnant.
The idea that a child was growing in her stomach, her own
child, made her comfortable with herself.
She had achieved very little in her short life and this felt like
one huge achievement.
A child of her own.
To do with her whatever she wanted.
This was something to be proud of.
She was looking forward to the birth of her child.
Then Sarah was born and a lot of things changed in
Therezia's life.
She slowly came to realize that having a child did not just end
at giving birth to one.
There was a lot more to it.
The idea of further education for her, kind of disappeared.
Partly due to the social stigma that went together with a
teenage pregnancy, partly because she had to work to cover
the costs.
She did not mind.
Therezia was never too good at school anyway, and, growing

up with a working mother she got used to doing the washing and the ironing.

And the two women working together were quite successful at their work. Then her mother passed away and Therezia was alone with Sarah.

She did not mind that either.

She was used to working. She actually enjoyed it.

The washing and ironing occupied her hands and her mind was free to roam.

Whilst she was working, she forgot about things.

No body aches. No pains in the mind.

No feelings of shame or loneliness.

Her only connection to this world was Sarah.

She was a lovely girl.

When she cuddled her, everything felt okay.

She had this magical ability of bringing peace to everyone she touched.

If only they could have a conversation.

If only they could understand each other.

The rest of the world was absolutely irrelevant.

Sarah was enough to keep her completely occupied.

Often strange things happened around her. Like last week for example, when a bunch of kids came running to her house.

"Mrs Rodriguez! Mrs Rodriguez! Come quickly! Some boys took Sarah's teddy bear away and threw it over the fence to where that big black dog is. She is trying to climb the fence to get her teddy bear. Please come quickly. That dog is very nasty."

That dog did indeed have a bad reputation. Just a few months ago it ripped the mailman's leg open.

When anyone walked past, it hurled itself against the fence trying to get to them.

THE PSI WARS

Therezia arrived completely out of breath in front of the house. Leaning against the fence trying to catch her breath, she looked in amazement at the sight before her.

Lying next to Sarah, with its huge paw on her lap was the black dog with that terrible reputation.

With its eyes closed obviously enjoying Sarah rubbing the top of its head.

Therezia could swear that it was purring.

The owner of the dog , having also just arrived was looking astonished at the scene before him.

This had never happened before.

That dog was specially trained to be vicious, to guard and protect the house.

He got rid of Sarah and her mother very quickly.

He did not want his dog to learn to be nice.

Sarah loved her mother.

She loved to touch her, to cuddle her.

To breathe in her smell.

She spent hours just sitting and watching her mother work.

The washing, the ironing, fascinated her.

She could not quite grasp the meaning of the activity, but loved to see her mother doing it.

She could nearly understand what she was doing.

Nearly.

Her mother was not like other people.

Other people were completely foreign to her.

The things they did.

The noises they made with their mouths.

Her mother was different.

She could nearly understand her.

What she was doing, what she was saying.

Those things were more familiar.

Sarah felt that just with a bit of extra concentration, just with a bit more observation, she could grasp the meaning. It was so close. She could nearly get there.

Nearly.

Therezia had very similar feelings.

She loved her daughter.

When she cuddled her, it left a deep peace within her.

When she was near, everything felt just right.

Of course, she often wished that Sarah would be like other children.

Wished that she had friends and would get together with other families.

But when she cuddled Sarah in her arms and buried her face into that golden mass of hair, she would not have changed anything.

They were happy together.

She could watch her daughter and be content with what she saw.

For her those eyes were not as blanks as when Sarah looked at other people.

For Therezia those eyes had depth, had meaning.

There was a deep intelligence in those eyes trying to break through to the surface.

It almost made it.

Almost.

She kept watching her daughter trying to understand her.

Trying to understand what went on inside that head of hers.

Trying to understand all that activity that appeared to be going on inside, separated from the outside by that blank wall.

She felt she just had to reach out and see what was inside.

Sometimes she felt she nearly made it.

Nearly.

....

Therezia sat up in bed with her eyes wide open in fright.
The Call.
Yes, it was the same call, she was sure about it, although she
had not heard the voice for many years.
Since well before Sarah was born.
She just about forgot the whole thing.
But now it was back.
She was sure it was the same call.
That deep, soft voice in her mind.
She was woken up by it many times in the past.
Calling her, telling her things.
Therezia could not remember any details. It was a long time
ago.
But it was the same voice, of that, she was sure.
Therezia tried to concentrate, to remember.
She was sure there was more to that voice.
Something important. Things she ought to remember.
She tried, yet she could not remember anything else.
There was something about that voice in her mind.
The same voice, although...there was a difference this time.
Difference....Therezia felt that this was important.
She tried to concentrate.
The difference....oh, yes. This time it was not calling her.
Sarah!
Therezia jumped out of bed and ran to her daughter's room.
Sarah was sitting up in her bed, eyes wide open with a
perplexed expression on her face.
"So you heard it too?"—Therezia stated the obvious.
Of course she heard it. That call would have felt like a
battering ram in her mind.
Therezia remembered quite well the first time she got the call.

9

It was very hard to accept the reality of that voice in her mind. So how would Sarah react?

There was no possible way she could understand what was happening.

Her maternal instinct was telling her that she had to protect Sarah.

But how?

And why?

She could not remember anything bad associated with the voice.

Yes, it was demanding and ordering, but always in a kind, friendly way.

And the things the voice was telling her were always.....well, she just could not remember the things the voice had been telling her.

Still, this need for protection was very strong inside her.

"Sarah! Listen carefully. The next time you hear that voice call me. You understand? It is very important."

Those deep eyes looked into hers unblinkingly, nearly understanding.

Nearly.

Therezia grabbed her daughter's shoulders and shook the girl.

"Sarah! This is very important!"

Her mother had never attacked her before.

Sarah understood violence and this, coming from her mother was very frightening.

She started to cry.

This in turn frightened her mother. She could not remember Sarah crying before.

Ever.

Not even when she was a baby.

What did she do to her? How could she have upset this
innocent soul so much?

Therezia cuddled her daughter and pulled her hard against
her.

She buried her face in her daughter's hair and cried with her.

It actually felt good.

They were crying there together for a long time until they both
fell asleep.

....

The next morning everything appeared normal.

Therezia was doing the ironing in the kitchen and Sarah
looked happy in her favourite corner, watching her mother
work.

On the surface.

Deep inside, Therezia was nothing even remotely like normal.

That Call of the previous night brought to the surface long
forgotten emotions. Things she had not thought about for
many years.

That Call filled her with fear.

Fear for Sarah.

The strange thing was that Therezia could not remember
anything bad related to that Call.

She had only nice memories about that voice, still, her gut
feeling told her that she should protect Sarah.

What was not clear to her, though, was not just why she
should protect her, but also how to do it.

How do you protect against a voice booming in your head?

The good thing was that Sarah probably did not remember the
whole thing by now.

However – Therezia was wrong in that .

Very wrong.

Sarah remembered every bit of last night's events.

It took her by surprise at first, but the real surprise came shortly thereafter.

That call, that sound had a meaning for her.

Never before could she relate to the noises people made with their mouths.

Not even when her own mother spoke to her. Most of the time she deduced the meaning from her body language.

Her mother sometimes believed that she had got through to her, but it was mainly guess work on Sarah's part.

Spoken words had no meaning for her.

But this Call was different.

It went right through, right inside.

It had a meaning. It carried a message.

And she understood it.

The first sound she had ever understood.

And it was friendly. It was nice.

She could never forget about that voice.

Sarah hoped it would come again tonight.

. . . .

That night both mother and daughter went to bed early but neither could fall asleep for a long time.

For different reasons, but both of them were waiting for the Call.

They stayed awake as long as they could but the Call did not come.

The following night, just as they had given up waiting, the Call came.

Strong and demanding.

Therezia rushed to Sarah's room to find a completely unexpected picture; Sarah was sitting on her bed with a smile on her face. Her eyes were bright, full of understanding. From the gestures she made, she was obviously listening to something her mother could not hear.

Therezia picked her daughter up in a strong hug and dragged her to the kitchen where she washed Sarah's face with cold water, rubbed her back and talked into her ear to get her away from the voice.

"Leave my daughter alone!" she shouted into the dark night.

The answer thundered back like a slap on the face.

"Therezia, we have no ill will towards you or your daughter. You had a child for a reason, a purpose.

Now it is Sarah's turn to fulfil her destiny."

"What destiny? What do you mean? Leave her alone!"

There was no answer.

The night was silent, cold and dark.

Sarah started to cry clinging to her mother, more from the disappointment of losing the Voice, than for any other reason

It took Therezia a long time to calm her down.

....

The next four nights were very hectic for both of them.

The Call came relentlessly every night. Sometimes twice a night and Therezia had a hard time trying to interrupt the communication with Sarah.

Sarah herself was very confused about the whole thing.

She normally had a hard time adjusting to new things in her life and this repeated interruption sometimes left her really confused.

She did not complain when the Call came.

She did not complain when her mother interrupted the communication.

She was not sure what to do, just allowed things to happen around her.

Therezia, on the other hand, carried more the burden of these things.

She was constantly tense, alert, in order to be ready to jump in and help Sarah when the need arose.
She was still not clear about the reason why Sarah needed her help but she just followed her instincts.
Her gut feeling told her that the Call was not as friendly as it appeared to be, and Sarah needed her protection.
So she did her best.
Then suddenly, the peace returned.
The Call did not come any more.
No warnings, no obvious reasons for it to suddenly stop coming just as there did not appear to be any reason for it to start.
It just stopped.
Their daily routine slowly returned to normal although a long time passed before either of them could have a good night sleep.
Therezia was happy that the Call was not coming any more, she felt safer. She felt that Sarah was safer.
For Sarah it was a bit harder to get over those bizarre nights.
She was really confused about the whole thing.
The sudden appearance of the voice, the first one she had ever truly understood.
The obvious distress of her mother and her frantic efforts to stop it.
And the sudden disappearance of that voice leaving her again alone when she hoped for its company.
The experience changed Sarah.
She did not want to leave the house anymore.
She preferred to sit in her favourite corner in the kitchen and just watch her mother work.
All day long.
Therezia did not mind it at all.

Partly because now she did not have to worry about where her daughter was, and partly because she liked her company. Actually, she felt so alone that she would have loved anybody's company but with Sarah it was different.

It was nice to talk to someone knowing that it didn't matter what you said as the only answers you would get, came from your own imagination.

Sarah was safe to talk to.

She just listened, looking at her with those large, blank looking eyes, smiling at her no matter what she was telling her.

Therezia was so busy with her own feelings that for a long time she did not notice the changes in Sarah.

Until Sarah started to talk.

Well not quite talk but rather she began whispering to herself. It took Therezia several weeks to notice this change, probably because it happened so slowly. So gradually.

She just sat in her corner with her head bent down whispering to herself.

As Therezia noticed, and began to observe, the whispering was not just a few words here and there. There were long conversations.

She said something – then was quiet for a while as though listening for an answer, then she was talking again. Judging by the changing expressions on her face and the movements of her hands, she was having a very vivid conversation with someone.

"Sarah talking to someone – nonsense"- she corrected herself.

One day when Therezia was quite tired after washing a big load, she sat down next to her daughter to rest for a while. With her arm around Sarah's shoulder she pulled her close and asked her jokingly.

"Who are you talking to pumpkin?"

"I am talking to Carlos."

It was lucky that Therezia was sitting, otherwise who knows what would have happened.

Sarah understood her question.

And answered.

Clearly and loudly.

This was not her Sarah.

Sarah could never answer her like that.

She must be hallucinating.

"Did you just talk to me?"

Sarah just nodded her head. She clearly understood the question.

"But.....but how....you have never before...."

"Carlos said that the problem was in my head. Something not connecting. He fixed it up for me."

"In your head?"

Sarah just nodded again. Her eyes were clear, expressive, understanding and connecting.

"He fixed it up? In your head?"

Sarah just nodded again.

"Did it hurt?"

"A little bit"

"I still can't understand . I am very happy that you can talk and we can understand each other but I don't get it. All the doctors assured me that this just could not possibly happen."

"They did not know how to fix it."

"And this Carlos knows?"

"He knows many things."

"Could I talk to this Carlos?"

Sarah took her mother's hand and put it on her stomach.

"Talk to him."

"What do you mean? Why should I touch your stomach?"

"That is where Carlos is."

Therezia froze for a minute. Then the fear was obvious on her face when she grasped the meaning of her daughter's words.

"Carlos says that you should take me to a doctor."

....

Yes, the pregnancy was confirmed and yes, Dr Kovellsky had a lot of questions and comments.

"You do understand Therezia that I have to report this to the authorities?"

"I did not know that you have to report pregnancies."

"Not pregnancies – teenage pregnancies. She is under age and pregnant. This is against the law."

"And who will you charge with the felony?"

"The father naturally. By the way who is he?"

"Dr Kovellsky, if you ask me the same bunch of questions that you did seventeen years ago, you will get the same bunch of answers. You did not believe me then, and you will not believe me now."

"So you insist that Sarah has never been with a man?"

"You took the words right out of my mouth."

"Sorry Therezia, I just cannot accept that. You were pregnant, now she is pregnant. Those babies got there somehow and sorry, but I do not believe in Immaculate Conception or any other miracles."

"Then Doctor you'd better sit down because I will show you a miracle which will rock your socks off."

"What are you talking about?"

"Just sit down, trust me, you will need to."

"Okay. I am sitting. Now what are you talking about?"

"Please ask Sarah how she knew that she was pregnant?"

"Are you joking?"

"No, I am very serious."

"Therezia, you know very well that Sarah not only won't be able to answer me but could not even understand the question."

"Doctor, just humour me and ask her the question"

"Okay, Sarah please tell me. How did you know that you were pregnant?"

"Carlos told me."

The smile froze on the doctor's face.

He did not move. He did not make a sound.

For a long time he just stared at Sarah.

After quite a few minutes, as though waking up from a dream, he jumped to his feet and faced Therezia.

Really angry.

"Okay Therezia, how did you do it? Did you learn ventriloquism or is it an electronic gadget?

How did you do this trick? I really don't feel like jokes today."

"You are a doctor. Examine the patient and make a diagnosis."

"Are you testing me? Okay, I will go along with you. Sarah could you stand up and come here please. Thank you. Now show me your left ear. Thank you. Now open your mouth and stick your tongue out. Thank you. Now just go back to your chair and sit down."

The doctor sat down heavily behind his desk. He had a completely befuddled expression on his face.

"She does understand me. You can't fake that, but it is not possible. She could not....."

"Sarah who is Carlos?"

"The baby in my stomach."

"How do you know that his name is Carlos?"

"He told me."

"You can talk to him?"

"Of course."

"How come you can suddenly talk? You could not before?"

"There was something wrong in my head. Carlos fixed it."

"What did he do to you?"

"I am not sure. He told me but it was too complicated. I did not really understand it all."

Dr Kovellsky, still with that confused expression on his face lifted the phone on his desk.

"Mrs Perez please ask the other doctors to come to my office. Yes, all three of them and right now."

There was silence in the room for a few minutes until there was a knock on the door and the three doctors entered. Two young men and a middle aged female.

"Therezia, these are my partners Dr Gutierez and Dr Misha and the lady is Dr Markins. You have probably met them before."

Then turning to the doctors.

"Sorry to interrupt your routine but there is something here I would like you to see, partly because I need witnesses to confirm what is happening, partly I just want to know that I am still sane and not hallucinating.

You are all familiar with Sarah here. You know her diagnosis and you know her disabilities. Am I right?"

The lady doctor was the first to talk.

"Her diagnosis is on her face. Those features are diagnostic to Down's syndrome and we all know the limited mental capacities which go with it. I think we can all agree with that."

"Well....yes. Except..."

"Yes Dr Misha?"

"Well, I think her mental capacities, and communication skills are much more limited than what you would expect with Down's syndrome. Yes, she obviously has that but to explain the degree of incapacity she has, we have to consider also other congenital abnormalities beside Down's syndrome."

"Thank you Dr Misha. Your diagnosis completely coincides with mine. Now to complete this quest could you ask Sarah a question?"

"Doctor?"

"Please ask her a question. Any question."

"Are you sure?"

"Positive."

"You know that she will not understand the question, much less be able to answer it."

"Just ask her that damned question Doctor."

"Okay. Okay. Don't bite me. Well, Sarah tell me, how do you feel?"

"I feel fine doctor."

There was a stunned silence in the room. The doctors just looked at each other without being able to make a comment. Dr Kovellsky gave a very satisfying sigh.

"That is good. That is perfect. This at least proves that I am not mad or hallucinating. Please Doctors, examine Sarah and convince yourselves of the reality of what you are witnessing. I will need you all later to back me up because no one will believe this."

....

They got home quite late that night.

It was hard to get away from the doctors constant probing, questioning of Sarah. Therezia had to be quite rude to stop them, so they would let them go.

Sarah was very tired by that time but appeared to be enjoying being the centre of attention.

She was not used to talking to people, not used to understanding them and being understood by them. It was a completely new experience for her.

Therezia was more worried.

Although she was very much pleased by the sudden change in her daughter, she did not understand it, and she feared it. She related those changes to the Call and in her mind everything related to the Call was not necessarily a good thing.

Including this pregnancy business.

She clearly remembered now that she also came to be pregnant after the Call, although she could not imagine how one could get pregnant after listening to a voice.

Still the reality was that Sarah was indeed pregnant.

They had to deal with the situation.

Therezia remembered how hard it was for her to go through her pregnancy without the understanding of her mother and decided that this would not happen to Sarah.

She would stand by her side and help her through this pregnancy and after that, for as long as she was needed. In her mind she was already planning the things they could do together to make it easier for Sarah.

However, Carlos and the changes he appeared to cause in Sarah – those things she simply put out of her mind.

They were beyond her comprehension and thinking about them just got her confused.

She just wanted to concentrate on the things she was familiar with. She just wanted to go through this pregnancy and then face whatever would come next.

....

The pregnancy itself was advancing without any problems .Dr Kovellsky grudgingly admitted that there was nothing he had to do except keep his eye on the progress and just run the routine tests.

He was not very happy when Therezia declared that just one comment from him about the changes in Sarah would cause her to look for another doctor.

This was somewhat rude but it was the only way they could keep their peace of mind and still keep him as their doctor.

So he just looked after Sarah's health and nothing more.

Still, Therezia could not prevent him from observing Sarah, what she did, what she said, and from keeping very detailed notes about her progress.

At home Therezia was really enjoying her daughter's company, now that they could talk and tell each other their thoughts.

They talked for hours every day, especially at night before they went to bed.

They talked about everything.

The way they felt, the way they thought of the outside world.

Therezia had at last someone to talk to about her long years of loneliness in the company of a daughter she could not communicate with.

Sarah told her about the simple peacefulness of her quiet years without any interference from the outside world and then about the excitement of the recent weeks when it was like suddenly opening her eyes and seeing a completely different world, a world she could now relate to and even be a part of.

They talked for ages everyday but the subject of the Call or Carlos was very carefully avoided.

Both felt uncomfortable with things neither of them could understand and by an unsaid agreement both avoided those subjects.

They were able to do this although it was not easy and deep inside they both knew and felt their presence.

As far as Therezia was concerned it was just pure denial of a subject she could not understand and was afraid of.

For Sarah it was more complicated.

She could not deny Carlos and was not trying to.

She had long conversations with him when her mother was not around, especially at night.

Although these were very intense communications, they were very one sided as Sarah was mainly listening and learning.

Learning a lot of new wonderful things, things that Therezia could not have taught her.

Probably no one could.

....

Sarah's pregnancy was advancing absolutely perfect.

She started to show a bit of a belly now but no morning sickness or back aches or any other problems which would commonly go along with a pregnancy.

Dr Kovellsky confirmed a male pregnancy.

Mother and daughter were closer to each other with every passing day – so everybody was happy.

Except Dr Kovellsky as he felt that he was robbed of the chance to study something extraordinary, something that comes along only once in a lifetime.

Therezia could have been happy and should have been happy but she was afraid.

And she was getting more and more afraid every day.

She had no logical reason to be afraid but she had the growing gut feeling that something was about to happen, something she would not like at all.

This absolute perfection of everything just could not last.

Sooner or later something would happen that would break all

this perfectness.

Still, nothing wrong appeared on the horizon.

Sarah showed her a few little tricks that remarkably increased her speed of washing and ironing.

She was able to comfortably do a much larger amount of work and with Sarah's help the business boomed.

She was able to take a few days off and have a rest.

They had more time to spend together as Sarah's tummy was

slowly getting bigger.Sarah kept her excited with new surprises practically every

day.

Like the other day when she looked into Sarah's room at night and found her reading a book.

In the past the whole idea would have been ridiculous. Today Therezia accepted the idea as normal, though she expected the book to be a child's picture book.

Instead, her daughter was reading about caesarean sections.

"When did you learn to read?"

"I....I don't know. I thought I always knew how to, . I just opened a book and started to read."

"And why are you reading about this particular subject?"

"Well, Carlos told me I would probably need one. He said I've got a very narrow pelvis and he would be probably too big to come through naturally. He was very sorry but said that there was nothing anyone could do about."

"Isn't it something dangerous?"

"Well it is a bit of a risky operation but many women have had it in the past with no problems."

"We'd better talk to Dr Kovellsky about this."

"And what will you tell him, how will you explain your knowledge about it?"

"I will just tell him that this problem runs in our family and that

I am worried. I will ask him to run some tests just to make me feel better."

....

Dr Kovellsky of course confirmed the problem.

He said that he knew about the disproportion between Sarah's pelvis and the expected size of the baby but also that there was nothing anyone could do about it.

The present attitude was to wait and see.

He also confirmed another problem.

Sarah had a congenital malformation of the uterine arteries which was very good for the baby as it vastly increased the blood supply to the placenta, increasing with that the baby's nourishment, but it also made the potential caesarean section more dangerous.

With so many dilated blood vessels around, a very large bleeding during operation was a possibility.

He also said that there was nothing to worry about for now.

They would cross that bridge when they came to it.

For Therezia this was the disaster she was expecting all along.

The bad news that would interrupt the happy flow of events.

The idea that Sarah would not be around, not be part of her life was completely unacceptable to her.

She dragged Sarah from specialist to specialist but the general opinion did not change.

Be ready for anything but for now just wait and hope.

With a bit of luck she might get away with a natural birth.

Therezia did not believe this.

Her gut feeling did not allow it but there was nothing else she could do.

She put on a happy face for Sarah and went along with their life as usual.

But inside her, there was this growing fear of the approaching birth.

Sarah was happy.

She was able to help her mother quite a lot in her work and would spend the days smiling and singing to herself.

By that time she was starting to walk leaning back slightly as her stomach was getting quite large.

Still, she had no pain, no discomfort.

It was an ideal pregnancy.

As her due date was getting closer Dr Kovellsky put her in hospital two weeks early to get everything ready, to be prepared for all possibilities.

At this stage the caesarean section appeared unavoidable.

Therezia spent every day with her daughter putting on a happy face in spite of the terror she was feeling inside.

She acted by instinct only, she could not think clearly.

She even went so far as asking Sarah what Carlos said about her not being around to look after her baby.

Sarah would not answer this which kind of confirmed her fear.

When her bed was pushed into the operating room she was smiling at her mother.

It was a goodbye smile.

CHAPTER TWO

Carlos was a large, very healthy baby.

His skin was a bit darker than her mother's and his large, black eyes were somewhat slanted.

So slightly, that you had to watch closely to notice.

And he never cried.

Therezia could not remember if she ever heard him crying.

He also slept very little .

He just lay quietly in his basket with hands touching everything he could reach and eyes following everything that moved.

He always accepted the food offered to him but never asked to be fed.

Therezia had to go by guessing when to feed him, when to change him, when to wash him. It was just lucky that she had been through this before and she knew what to do.

Taking care of a baby's physical needs was almost automatic to her. But this time around, it was all different.

This time, she had a baby with eyes beaming with understanding.

This time she had a baby she was proud to show off.

There were a lot of young and not so young women with small children in the neighbourhood and she was welcomed by them.

She met them, she invited them to her home and she was invited by them. Suddenly she had a lot of friends, was involved in many activities.

Just the way it was supposed to happen before, but did not.

With this child she was welcomed everywhere.

She had put away a bit of money when business was going so well, before Carlos was born and she also had some

government help, as she was bringing up the child alone.
So she did not have to work so hard and she had plenty of
time to socialize.
All this was like having a second chance in life.
And Carlos was growing.
Fast.
All the usual milestones, like lifting his head, turning around,
getting up on his feet – all of them happened much earlier
than they were supposed to.
By four months he had a few teeth out and Therezia was quite
happy that she did not have to breast feed him.
From the very early few months Carlos understood Therezia's
simple commands and quite happily responded to them.
However, he was quite late in starting to talk.
By eight months he had an array of facial expressions and
had signals to indicate what he wanted but was well over two
years old when he started to talk.
However, when he did start, he spoke full sentences, not just
words like other children.
When he started to talk it was.....well...
It was his second birthday.
Therezia organised a nice birthday party for him inviting a
bunch of kids with their mothers.
They all had a lot of fun.
After a while the mothers retired to a corner of the room,
talking and just watching the children.
They were a boisterous group.
Running, jumping around climbing up on top of everything,
making a mess on the floor, throwing food all over each other.
And Carlos was there right in the middle.
He was starting things, inventing the mischief and the other
kids followed him.

Everyone was noisy and shouting.

Except Carlos.

In the middle of all that activity no sound left his mouth.

Everyone noticed this, but Therezia was not worried.

She had taken Carlos to several specialists because of his lack of speech and all said the same thing.

There was nothing wrong with the child.

She was told to just leave him alone. He would start talking when he was ready.

That night Therezia got to bed quite late. It took a long time to clean up all that mess but she did not mind.

She and Carlos were accepted, were part of the local community.

They had friends. They had a social life.

She had not realised until then, how much she missed all of that.

....

In the middle of that night Therezia woke up with a fright.

The Call!!

She ran into Carlos's room picked him up and started to drag him into the kitchen to wash his face, trying to interrupt the call.

And that was when Carlos spoke for the first time.

"It is alright mother. Don't worry. Everything is OK."

The sound of that soft voice was like a bucket of cold water on her. At first she thought she was hearing the Call.

"Did you say something Carlos?"

"Yes mother. I can speak just choose not to. Please do not worry about that Call. They do not wish me any harm."

"Every time the Call came in the past something bad happened. I don't want anything to happen to you."

"Nothing bad will happen to me. I promise you. Those people

outside are friends of mine and just want to talk to me."
"What people outside. Why don't they come in?"
"Most of them are very far away."
"I.... I am confused. Everything was so nice until now, but again things are happening I do not understand. You were a nice, normal boy, like any other child. We had a nice normal life like everyone else. Now I have a two year old boy who talks like an adult and who talks to some friends who just happen to be very far away. What is happening to me?"
"Mother, listen to me. Let me explain things the best I can. I am a two year old boy with a two year olds thoughts, wants, and behaviours. But at the same time I am also something else. I can't explain that part of me any better to you as I myself am not sure what that something is. I would prefer if you could both accept and ignore this other part of me as I would not like to keep secrets from you. What I would really like is if you could look after the two year old me just as before and to try to ignore my other part, no matter how strange it might appear to you.
Do you think you can do that?"
"I don't know. I am confused. It is too sudden."
"Mother, we will have a lifetime together for you to get used to it. Just always remember one thing, that I love you!."
"Carlos, that is the magical word that can make anything happen."

....

So they came to an agreement and Therezia kept her part of it. She kept looking after her two year old boy like any mother would do.
She fed him, washed him and played with him.
Took him to the park to play with other children while she enjoyed the company of their mothers.

THE PSI WARS

And Carlos was behaving like any other two year old.
He was running, shouting and climbing with the other children.
The other children liked him as he was always inventing and
doing interesting things and followed him.
Like the other day when the mothers noticed that all the
children instead of running around were sitting on the ground
in front of a large crack on the wall.
They were clapping, pushing each other, shouting and
giggling. The mothers were happy as they seemed to have
fun in a more quiet way.
What they did not hear was what they were saying.
"Come out birdie, come out."
They also did not see the large seagull that emerged from the
hole in the wall dragging one of its wings on the floor.
The children all shouted and giggled when it came to them
and all wanted to touch it.
And the bird let them.
It went straight to Carlos and put its head in his lap.
It didn't move even when Carlos put the broken wing back in
place and kept his hand on it as though trying to warm it up.
The mothers only became aware that something was
happening when the children started shouting and when they
saw a large seagull circling above them.
They ran to the children in panic only finding them rolling on
the floor pushing each other, laughing, all happy that they
were playing with the bird.
And so, Therezia was doing her part of bringing up a two year
old and at the same time was doing her best to ignore the
"other part".
And it really was not easy for her.
Trying to ignore the Call, for example.
Therezia tried putting her pillow over her head so as not to

hear it, but how do you block out a voice that is inside your head.

Although on the one hand she did not really mind that Carlos's "other part" was not alone, that it had some sort of guidance which she was not able to provide, she could not overcome her maternal fear and distrust of the Call.

Still, Carlos appeared to be happy listening to the voices nearly every night.

He said to Therezia that the voices were teaching him about who he really was.

At this point Therezia usually changed the subject.

She did not want to know any more about that side of things. She felt safer sticking to the part she understood and just denied the rest.

Carlos was growing up in a more or less normal household, well accepted as a normal boy in the neighbourhood.

Everything was smooth and happy until he got old enough to go to school.

By that time he was taller than the other kids, very slim with a long oval face.

He had very black hair which he wanted to wear long but Therezia put her foot down.

"You do not want to look like a girl?"

At first Carlos refused to go to school. He maintained that he didn't need to.

Therezia had to be very convincing again.

She pointed out that by not going to school he would have to go through a lot of legal hurdles as attending school was required by law.

Besides he would be better off not calling attention to himself. He would not want to appear different in other people's eyes.

That was a good argument. So Carlos went to school.

....

"Rodriguez! Carlos Rodriguez!"

"Yes Miss."

"Are you listening?"

"Yes Miss, I am listening."

"You are not looking at me."

"I am listening with my ears Miss."

"Okay smarty pants. From now on I want you to listen with your ears and I want you to be looking at me with your eyes at the same time. Is that clear?"

"Yes Miss."

Carlos had been going to school only for a few days but he already began to dislike it.

There were rules for everything.

How to sit, how to walk and how not to run in the corridors.

He could not talk during class.

He even had to ask permission to go to the toilet.

Still all this would have been acceptable if not for the sheer dullness of the classes... they were so boring!

They had not even got to the beginning of writing yet.

It was pure luck that his teacher noticed his behaviour and realised that he did not belong in that class. She took him to the headmaster and after a long time and a lot of questions, they decided that based on his general knowledge he should skip to the fourth grade.

Which appeared to be fine to everyone.

Therezia was up on cloud nine, telling anyone and everyone she could that Carlos began school in the fourth grade as he was too smart for the others.

His teacher was quite content about this "experiment", she was even going to write a paper about it.

Only Carlos wasn't very sure about things.

On the one hand, classes got more interesting as he was now actually learning new things.

But on the other hand he was three years younger than the rest of his classmates which created a whole new set of problems.

It is never good to be the youngest and the smallest in a pack.

Not amongst animals, but especially not amongst humans.

And especially not amongst school children who can be the most vicious of the lot.

Carlos, who although tall for his age, was the ideal target for all the bullies in his class.

The worst of them was Zoltan who was the largest and noisiest of all the kids.

He was a big one alright. His father was a professional boxer, not a particularly successful one, but good enough to make a reasonable living for his family.

Zoltan grew up in a violent, physically oriented environment which he naturally applied to his school life.

He really enjoyed upsetting his school mates.

With a bunch of similarly minded followers he roamed the school yard during free periods, pushing the kids around, taking their lunch money away or simply just hitting them when it was least expected.

The skinny, much younger and weaker looking boy was the perfect target for them. They followed him around and got more and more upset as the young kid did not seem to be afraid of them like all the others.

They called him names, shoved his books out of his hands and tripped him to make him fall.

Carlos would just get up from the floor, calmly collect his books and kept going, ignoring the insults and laughter all around.

After a while the bullies got fed up with this lack of reaction.
Zoltan stood in front of Carlos with his legs apart blocking his
way.

"Hey skinny. What do you think of my shoes?"

Carlos was trying to get away but his way was blocked left
and right.

"Well skinny, when I ask you a question I expect an answer.
What do you think of my shoes?"

"They are dirty."

"Exactly. I want you to clean them."

"I have to go."

"Not until you have cleaned my shoes."

Carlos just stood there while all the others were laughing
around him.

Zoltan was putting on a show for the rest of them.

"This kid is very reluctant to clean my shoes. He needs to be
taught a lesson."

He lunged at Carlos, grabbing him by the throat and pulled
him very close to his face.

"Now"- grinning into his face -"What are we doing about my
shoes?"

Carlos did not move nor did he respond.

With both hands down by his side holding his books, he just
looked into Zoltan's eyes. No one else but Zoltan saw the
purple flame in his eyes.

Everything froze for a while. Zoltan holding Carlos by the
neck.

Carlos without moving a muscle looking at his eyes.

The rest around them just holding their breath waiting for
something to happen.

After a long time without moving, Zoltan let go of Carlos's
neck, and just resting his hand on his shoulder declared to the

others.

"This kid is alright. Better no one dare touch him."

From then on Carlos had no further problems.

Zoltan followed him everywhere, making sure that nobody bothered him.

At first it was a bit of a nuisance, but Carlos got used to the persistent company and learned to ignore it.

It was a good ending for everyone.

Carlos was left in peace to do whatever he wanted.

Zoltan was too busy to go bullying anyone.

The rest of the bullies lost interest after missing their leader.

The school yard had never been this quiet before.

....

"From now on I will believe in miracles"- Mrs Tranders slowly lowered her voluminous body into the creaking, protesting chair.

"You would not believe what I have just seen."

There were four other teachers in the room. It was lunchtime and the teachers enjoyed the rest period as much as the students did.

"What did you see?"

"You would not believe me. Guess who I just saw sitting on the stairs reading a book?"

"Who?"

"Zoltan."

"Go away."

"No, really. I could not believe it myself. Had a good look just to make sure. It was Zoltan alright."

"Actually reading or just holding a book?"

"Reading. With his finger tracing the words and his lips moving. He was reading alright."

"I was not sure that he could read."

"He can. barely, but he can."

"Was he alone?"

"You know that lately he is never alone. He was with that strange new kid. He was reading too."

"That is not news. He is always reading"

"Or asking questions. Always asking questions. Of all sorts. Yesterday he asked me why I was wearing shoes when they were hurting my feet."

"And what did you say?"

"Well on the spur of the moment the only thing I could think of saying was that it would not be nice for me to go barefoot in the school. I still don't know how he knew that they were hurting me."

"I still do not know what to think about him."

"He is a nice kid – in a strange way."

"Strange is a word well used here. Look, after nearly thirty years of teaching these kids I pride myself in knowing my students. I just have to observe one for a few minutes and I know whether he is smart or stupid, if he is worth the effort to teach or just that he should be left alone as he would never get anywhere. But this youngster, well, I just can't put him in any of my pigeon holes."

"I have a problem placing him too. Sometimes he is like a sponge absorbing every bit of information, asking questions, reading books and other times he just sits there with vacant eyes as though listening to something from far away."

"He is reading alright. Last week I checked with the librarian the list of books he borrowed from the library. I tell you, I would be happy if my seventh graders would read those books."

"He can be a bit of a pest too. Yesterday as I was telling the class that besides the sun the most important thing for the

plants was rain. He reminded me that last week I said that
it was the wind because it brought the rain."
"Yes, you have to be careful what you say in front of him.
Sometimes I get the impression
that I am talking to two people . A nice five year old kid
standing in front of me, but then looking at his eyes there
seems to be another, a much older person inside. Sometimes
I get confused not knowing what language to use with him."
....

Carlos was walking home from school. It was a bit late, as he
had stayed back with Zoltan to discuss the math they had
learned that day.
That was no problem.
He walked home every day as the school was only a few
blocks away from his street. His backpack was a bit heavy as
he had taken quite a few books out of the library today but
it was not too bad.
The street was quiet with very few people around.
It was like a usual day – well, nearly.
Today he was afraid.
Carlos had been afraid many times before.
Like the first day at school, when he had to face the bullies,
and when the teachers questioned him.
But those were little fears. Nothing to get really upset about.
Today was different.
The fear was heavy, like having a big stone on his chest.
His legs did not want to work, for some reason they did not
want to go home. He had to force them to walk.
And yet, there was nothing around to be afraid of.
It was a strange feeling, like something absolutely dreadful

was about to happen.

At a very slow pace, with his head down, Carlos pushed on.

He felt stupid. There was nothing to be afraid of.

Still the fear was getting stronger as he was getting closer to home.

When he turned the corner into his street the fear hit him full force in the face.

Gasping for air, he was unable to move.

Not very far in front of him there was a big, black hole in the middle of the pathway.

Carlos was sure that hole had not been there before.

There were wisps of black smoke coming from the hole and there was a stench of something burning in the air.

Then he heard the growling.

Scratching noises and a deep growling sound was emerging from the hole. Something was moving in that hole.

The growling sound was like that of a big, very vicious dog.

Carlos was paralysed with fear.

He wanted to run away but was unable to move.

He just stood there, staring at that hole.

Watching that big black paw appear on the edge.

Then another one.

Then a long black snout with huge, curved, yellow teeth.

The red eyes were looking directly at him as the beast emerged from the hole.

There was a crackling noise behind him and a red ball of fire hit the beast on the chest, which with a loud yelp was pushed back towards the hole.

Then came another one which pushed the animal right back into the hole.

When the third one hit the hole, it just closed.

Once again, there was a smooth, uninterrupted footpath in

front of Carlos.

And he could move now.

The heavy fear just disappeared.

He turned around to face his saviour.

The tall woman dressed all in black appeared very old judging by her hair and her face, but stood quite straight and moved with great agility.

"Hello Carlos, nice to see you face to face."

Carlos smiled back at her recognising one of the voices which had been regularly visiting him at night.

"Thank you for getting rid of that, whatever it was."

"It was a drogan, a nasty creature that usually stays down in the deep. Come on, let's sit on that bench and talk."

Taking Carlos by the hand she led him to the nearby bench. Her hand was unusually warm.

"Carlos, I realize that you are only five and a half years old but I also know that you can understand at a level other kids of your age would not be able to. This thing which has just happened was not accidental and it may happen again. You were born with a purpose in your life and there are people around who would do anything to stop you from reaching your destiny. But there also are a lot people who are working very hard to protect you and to prepare you for your task. That is the main object for the voices that you hear at night, to teach you what you need to know. Here, please put this ring on your middle finger."

The ring was beautiful. It was formed by the coils of a black snake with red crystals for eyes.

"It is very big."

"Just put it on."

On his finger the snake came alive, lifting its head, it looked at him with its crystal eyes, then the coils tightened around his finger and it became a perfect fit.

A black metallic snake coiling around his finger.

"Please wear it all the time. If you feel in any kind of trouble, press on the snake with your thumb, and you will have help. Anywhere, or anytime, someone will come to offer help."

"Will you come to help me?"

"Sometimes me, sometimes someone else but you will never be alone."

With a squeeze of his shoulder, she disappeared around the corner, leaving Carlos looking after her quite confused.

Still, for some reason he felt extremely safe.

....

Therezia was happy with her life

She had no money problems, she had a lovely child and she had lots and lots of friends.

Her main occupation was looking after Carlos and she took the task very seriously.

She made sure that he always had the right alimentation, clean clothes and everything else she was able to give him.

And Carlos was a very well behaved child.

He loved his mother, always seeking her company. They were quite close to each other having long talks

regularly, just about everything.

The children of the neighbourhood loved to play with him, always asking their parents to take them where Carlos was.

They loved his friendly character and the way he always found something new and exciting to do.

Later on, when they were telling their mothers what they had done, how the fish in the pond were doing tricks for them or how the birds brought them fruits from the tops of the trees, the mothers just laughed.

What a fertile imagination their children had.

Just as the children were always around Carlos, their mothers were always around Therezia.

And she loved their company.

She loved her busy social life, the way they dropped in to see her, the way she was invited to their homes.

Everything was happy in her life.

At least during the day.

At night – there was the Call.

Therezia was trying to ignore her fears, but could never really accept the Call.

In her mind the Call was associated with bad things and she was worried about Carlos.

What did they want with her son?

Carlos was quite happy with his nightly visitors. He tried to tell his mother again and again that it was okay but he could not get rid of the fear in her mind.

He was trying to explain to her that the voices came from people who were his friends, who were trying to protect him and were teaching him important things.

That thanks to them he felt stronger and more secure and was feeling that he was growing inside, every day.

Therezia listened to what he was saying, nodding her head appearing to be in agreement, but Carlos knew that she could not accept the friendliness of the voices.

It was lucky that he did not appear to need much sleep as the mental visitors came nearly every night.

On those nights he was wide awake, listening, learning and practicing.

Therezia had no idea about the things that went on in his room. She tried to ignore the strange voices by putting her pillow over her head and never mentioned anything about the smells emanating from that room.

Still, every morning Carlos's room was clean and fresh as though nothing had gone on the night before.

It was like a non-verbal agreement between the two of them not to mention the things that went on in that room.

....

"Hello Carlos. It is nice to see you again."

Carlos smiled at the dark figure sitting on the edge of his bed.

"Hi Magda. It is nice to see you too, but if my mother sees you here she will freak out."

"She is asleep now."

"Did you make her sleep?"

"Well, kind of. She will wake up very rested in the morning."

"How come you came here?"

"I wanted to talk with you."

"You talked to me last night."

"That is different. Mental contact is okay when I teach you how to use your body's energies. When I want to have a conversation I prefer to do it face to face."

"Did I do anything wrong?"

"Why do you ask that?"

"Well, when people want to have a "conversation" with me it is usually when I have done something wrong."

"Good observation. You did not do anything really wrong but there are a couple of things I would like you to change."

"I knew it. I did upset you. I am sorry. What did I do wrong?"

"The things you do when you are playing with your friends."

"They all like it."

"Of course they do but you are not supposed to show people the things you can do."

"You told me to practice."

"Yes, but not in front of people."

"They were not people, just a bunch of kids."

"Yes, but they tell things to their mothers. Luckily so far no one has believed their stories but one day you might do something noticeable to an adult, and get yourself into a lot of trouble."

"What kind of trouble?"

"Remember when I told you that bad people are looking for you? Well, they do not know exactly who they are looking for, but they are searching for a boy who is able to do the things you can do. If people start talking about you, then they will find you."

"You will look after me won't you?"

"Of course I will, but it would be better if they did not find you. So please, do not do things in front of people, even if they are just kids."

"Okay, I won't."

"Is that a promise?"

"Okay, yes, but things will get very boring. They kind of expect me to do things."

"I am sure you can invent fun games without using your body energies."

"I will try but it was more fun the other way."

"I know it was, but this is important so please remember it. This doesn't mean I do not want you to keep practicing. I do, but not in front of people."

"Okay Magda."

"Thank you Carlos, now go to sleep."

The old woman touched Carlos's cheek with her warm hand and as he closed his eyes she slowly faded away into thin air.

....

Carlos was growing up.

44

Slowly or very fast depending of the observer.

For Therezia, he was still a little boy.

Loving, cuddly and well behaved. He made her happy.

Her only clues to his growing up were the changes in his room.

The large bunny rabbit poster on the wall was replaced by superman.

The pile of books growing in the corner. There was nowhere else to put them anymore.

There were books everywhere.

The number of large and small bottles all around the place full of insects, preserved animal bits and all sorts of other stuff.

The increasing number of gadgets on the table.

His prized possession was a small microscope which he won with his science project at school.

Carlos spent hours with that microscope, watching things moving around in pond water.

The noises, lights and smells that seeped through his closed door at night.

Therezia did not appear to notice these changes. Especially not the last ones.

Her mind was closed to Carlos's nightly activities.

They did not exist as far as she was concerned.

Every morning when she opened his door, Carlos was still asleep. The room clean and fresh, not a sign of what had been going on in there the night before.

And this was enough for her. She was happy with her son, herself, and her life in general.

....

At school Carlos was doing well.

Not exceptionally well, as he found some of the subjects absolutely boring, but well enough. All his teachers said that he could perform much better if only he would put more attention to his work.

Carlos spent a lot of time in front of the television like any other kid, but Therezia had the suspicion that he was not watching the programs. He was just staring into empty air – who knows what was going on in his head.

Therezia once switched the TV off in front of him. Carlos didn't even notice her doing so.

When these things happened Therezia just stayed clear of him. She felt very uneasy about this "other Carlos", the Carlos she could not understand.

She just concentrated on "her Carlos", then everything was well .

....

"Magda, when do I get my magic wand?"

"When do you get your what?"

"My magic wand."

'Carlos where did you get that idea from?"

"Well, all wizards are supposed to have a magic wand."

"And you are a wizard?"

"Well, what am I supposed to be?"

"Carlos, we have to have a serious talk. I know you are only seven years old.........."

"Seven and a half."

"Okay seven and a half. I think you are old enough to understand a few basic things. For a start, get the idea that you are a wizard out of your head."

"I am not?"

"No. You are not. Wizards do not exist. Magic does not exist. Magic wands, spells, potions – they are all for the movies and for children's stories."

"Then what is it that we are doing?"

"God, we should have had this talk long before now. Listen Carlos, you show an electric bulb to someone who has never seen one and it would appear to be magic. You explain to him how it works and it will stop being magic. It changes into knowledge. Magic and miracles are only things that you do not understand."

"But we are doing things............"

"Are you doing anything that you do not understand how does it works?"

"Of course not. If I did not know how it works, then I could not do it."

"Exactly. You are starting to see the light."

"But even if I would explain things to other people they could not do the things I am doing."

"You are right there, but it is still not magic. Let me explain a little further. Our brain is able to do fantastic things. For example, it produced some extensions that are able to perceive light so we could see."

"Our eyes?"

"Correct. Our brains also produced extensions to distinguish sound waves so we could hear."

"Ears?"

"Correct. Our brain also produced extensions of our body to be able to distinguish chemical particles so we can smell and taste."

"Nose, tongue. And I know the next one. You are talking about our five senses. The next one is touch. Still I can't see the connection between the five senses and magic."

"Just hold your horses! We have many more senses than these five, except that the other ones are not very common."

"What other ones?"

"For example some people have developed the capacity to

perceive electromagnetic waves on the frequency of mental activity. Some of them can hear thoughts. They are called telepaths."

"I heard about them."

"You heard about them! What the heck do you think that you are you doing when you are receiving your teaching at night?"

"Sorry I didn't think about that."

'Some people can feel other's emotions. They are called empaths. Some other people can manipulate heat waves. They can control fire and they are called pyrotechnics. Some other people are tuned into the wavelength of gravity. They can move objects without touching them. It is called telekinesis"

"That is neat. I would love to be able to do that."

"You have the capacity; you just haven't learned how to do it."

"When can I learn?"

"In time, when you are ready."

"I am ready now."

"Just let me decide when you are ready."

"Okay. I have to follow your advice but it still does not make any sense. I can see how when people do those things , they would appear as being magical to others. Still, the things you are teaching me do not seem to fit in anywhere."

"I am glad you are finally starting to use your head. Let me finish my explanation. There are also people, very few of them, whose mind developed the capacity to see the world in a different way.

They are able to see things not just as solid objects but can also be aware of the energy particles forming these objects. Please watch that table."

The small table in front of them slowly lost its sharp edges, began to sort of soften, to melt, and change shape.

In a very short time there was a solid chair standing in front of them.

Then again the chair started to melt and transformed itself back to being a table.

"Now Carlos, did I do magic?"

"No, you just rearranged the particles into a different order. I could do the same thing except my table would be much lumpier."

"That is just practice. Anyway, did you get my message? Do you still want your magic wand?"

"No thank you. I do not need a magic wand but I am not looking forward to the amount of learning I will have to do."

....

"Carlos, could I talk to you for a minute?"

"Of course Mum. What's up?"

"Do you have any plans for this coming Saturday?"

"No. Not really. Why?"

"A friend of mine is coming for lunch on Saturday. I would like you to meet him."

"Him? You only brought girls home so far."

"This is different. I met him a few times at the single parents group. He seems to be a nice person."

"You met him a few times at the group, then he comes for lunch?"

"Well. We have met a few times outside the group too. We had coffee together. We went for a walk on the beach. We always have a good time together."

"I am glad for you Mum. I was always wondering when you would stop being a nun."

"I have never been a nun. Anyway, so you are staying with us for lunch?"

"No problem. I will have lunch with you two then I will

disappear."

"That is not quite what I had in mind."

"Why? What do you want me to stick around for?"

"Well, Pietro, that is his name, has a daughter."

"So?'

"Her name is Moya. She is coming to lunch too."

"Mum. You want me to baby sit a girl?"

"Not babysitting. She is nearly nine just like you."

"But she is a girl."

"Yes, she is, but apparently a very nice one."

"Still, she is a girl."

"Carlos, you are not afraid of girls?"

"Not afraid. I just don't like them. Why can't she just go for a walk along the creek at the back of the house?"

"A very good idea. You can show her around."

"Mum!" ....

The lunch itself was a fairly enjoyable affair, partly due to the food which was very nice and partly due to the company. Therezia, as always, prepared just a few very simple dishes but they tasted fantastic.

There wasn't much food left on the table when they finished the meal.

Pietro was a tall, soft spoken man with very intense, dark eyes. When he looked at you you had the feeling that he could see everything inside you.

His thick, dark hair caused quite a lot of amusement for Carlos as he watched Pietro constantly trying to flatten it down, and the next minute it sprang up again pointing to the ceiling.

He talked clearly but with a strange, heavy accent which was quite nice to listen to.

Basically, Carlos's first impression of him was of a very nice man.

Moya, his daughter, however, was a completely different thing. She spoke politely when she had to, behaved quite lady like but at the same time she made it very obvious that she would have preferred to be somewhere else.

Her father on introducing her mentioned that she was an "acquired taste" and was quite correct in his statement.

She was dressed in elegant little girl's clothes with her dark hair in two long plaits.

The way she was constantly pulling on her clothes and tossing her hair made it clear that she felt uncomfortable with her appearance.

After a couple of glances in Carlos's direction she mainly kept her eye on her plate, pushing the food around but eating very little.

Carlos was quite relieved that he was being ignored by her as he did not really know what to talk about with a girl.

Their parent's attention was mainly on each other and they noticed only little about the unusual quietness of the children.

Lunch finished, the adults wanted to keep up their conversation so the children were told to get out and play outside.

Carlos was told to show Moya the neighbourhood.

For a good while they were walking quietly side by side, both trying and failing to find a reason to get away.

"What the hell is wrong with you?" Carlos could not hold it in anymore.

"And why do you think there is anything wrong with me?"- was the sharp answer.

"For starters you are a girl."

"You must be very smart to notice that."

"And I do not like girls."

"I do not like girls either."

This answer rattled Carlos a bit.

"But you are a girl."

"So?"

"So you do not like yourself?"

"I like myself. I just do not like being a girl."

"You would look funny as a boy."

"Why would I look funny?"

"A boy with long hair, dressed like a girl, playing with dolls."

"I do not play with dolls."

"All girls do. Having tea parties with dolls and giggling all the time."

"I do not do that."

"Don't you dress like a girl?"

"No, not if it were up to me what I wore. This dress was my father's idea to impress your mother."

"Still you are not boy material."

"Yeah? Just tell me what you can do better than me."

"The list would be too long to tell you now."

"Just tell me one thing."

Carlos got stuck here. He realised that he himself was not very good at the "boy things".

Football, running, fighting, swimming and all the usual boy things he was always trying to avoid.

He could not challenge Moya in reading a book.

Then he had an idea.

"You can't fish."

"I can catch more fish that you, anytime."

"Would you like to prove that?"

"When?"

"Right now."

"Okay, show me the spot but I didn't bring my gear."

"Not a good excuse. I got my stuff hidden at my fishing spot at the creek."

"Okay, let's go but if I catch more fish than what you do, you will accept that I would be good as a boy."

"If you catch more fish than I, I will accept that you are the King of England."

....

Carlos pulled out a plastic bag from its hiding place under a bush.

"You've got plenty of stuff in there to make up your own gear, providing that you know how to do it."

"Don't worry about me, but what about the rods?"

"We are using hand lines. You don't need rods where we are fishing from."

"Where is your fishing spot?"

"Right on the other side of that tree."

"There is water on the other side of that tree?"

"It is very hard to fish where there is no water."

"I am not getting into that water in this dress."

"You do not have to unless you fall into it. Just look at what is on the other side of that tree."

"Hey, Carlos, this is fantastic! This is the best fishing spot I have ever seen, providing there is fish in the water."

There was a long, thick branch which extended from the tree over the water nearly parallel to it, about four or five feet up. The perfect fishing platform.

"And what are you using for bait?"

"Now this is where those girly hands get dirty."

Carlos started to dig with his hands in the soft, moist ground between the roots of the tree.

In a few minutes he had a handful of fat, red worms squirming in his hand.

"Okay Moya, it is your turn. Get your hands dirty."

"I don't need to do that."

Moya went to a thick, half rotten tree trunk which was laying half in and half out of the water. With some effort lifted a large piece of loose bark. Three fat, white grubs fell to the ground. Carlos was impressed but did not show it.

"I have heard other kids using them but I have never tried them myself."

"You should have. They are good bait."

"So worms against grubs."

"I thought it was you against me."

"That is what I meant."

"Thank you for calling me a grub.

"That wasn't what.....oh cut it out!"

....

They were sitting side by side on the branch with legs hanging over the water, holding their fishing lines.

There was not much conversation as both concentrated on the water below them.

The water was quite deep at this point but was not clean enough to see what was under the surface.

They were sitting in the shade of the tree, still, the air was comfortably warm.

Carlos would have really enjoyed this perfect fishing afternoon – except for the company.

A girl.

Carlos couldn't make up his mind about Moya.

She was a girl, which was definitely against her. But at the same time, she did not act like a girl.

She obviously knew how to fish, she had no trouble climbing up the tree.

Other girls Carlos knew would not do those things.

Carlos nearly liked Moya.

If only she were not a girl.......

Carlos got a pull on his line.

Not very strong but it was definitely a fish.

And well hooked.

Carlos slowly pulled it up.

It was a nice silvery fish with a blunt nose, about the size of his hand.

It was a fish, a nice fish but not big enough to keep.

After flashing it a few times in front of Moya's eyes Carlos threw the fish back in the water.

"Worms one, grubs zero."

"Worms zero too."

"What do you mean, I just caught a fish."

"I can't see any fish."

"You saw me throw it back."

"Yes, you threw it back. You do not have a fish. That makes worms zero too."

"That is not fair and you know it. I will............"

There was a strong pull on Moya's line. She nearly lost her balance and fell into the water. Whatever was on her line, kept pulling strongly, trying to get away.

Carlos got really excited, completely forgetting the competition.

"Slowly, slowly, let it run. It is a big one. Do not lose it."

Moya knew what to do.

She slowly let her line out, then pulled it in.

They could not see what was pulling as it went quite deep, but Moya was bringing it slowly to the surface.

After a few times of Moya having to let the line out to prevent it from breaking, there was a disturbance on the surface of the water as her catch was trying to get away.

"What is that?"

"You caught a turtle."

Although it was pulling hard on the line, it was indeed a small turtle, with green moss covering its shell.

They managed to pull it up to the tree without breaking the line but it required four hands to remove the hook from the mouth of the fighting animal without being bitten.

It took a while before they let it jump out of their hands and with a big splash disappeared under the water.

"Worms zero, grubs one."

"I can't see any fish."

"My turtle was much bigger than your fish."

"And you threw it back."

"I did not throw it back. It jumped out of my hand."

"Whatever, you do not have it. Besides we are fishing here not turtling. It does not count.

Grubs zero."

"You are not fair! My turtle was.....hey, what is that?"

There was a long line of sharp sticks cruising on the surface of the water.

"Be quiet. Do not move a finger."

"What is it?"

"Those are the dorsal fins of a very big fish swimming just under the surface of the water."

"That big?"

"Yes. Don't move. It may come closer."

The spikes were heading straight towards them.

"Do not move" – Carlos whispered – "It's the king."

"King?"

"Shhhhhh"

It was a very large fish, nearly a metre long.

Dark green on top, large golden scales on the side.

His big tail moving slowly from side to side, it cruised along as though owning the water.

It passed right under them for a few metres, then, as though it had changed its mind, disappeared under the water.

"Did you see that?"

"Of course I saw it! You can't miss a thing that big. What did you mean by calling it the king?"

"That is just my name for it. I've seen this fish a few times before but when I told people about it, no one believed me. Not even my mother. At least I got a witness now."

"Who?"

"You."

"I am not sure I saw anything."

"Come on Moya, don't lie or I will push you into the water!"

"If I fall into the water you are coming in with me."

"Do you feel that strong?"

"Just try me."

As she jumped to her feet to defend herself her dress got caught on a small side branch. There was a loud ripping noise which made them both freeze.

"My father will kill me!"

"Turn around, let me have a look."

There was a long tear at one side of the back of her dress. Carlos concentrating slowly moved his hand above the tear. When he removed his hand , the tear was gone .

"It is okay. There is nothing wrong with your dress."

"But I heard...."

"Have a look for yourself!

With her dress intact Moya was much happier

."Carlos let's go home! Our parents are probably wondering where we are."

....

The children burst into the house nearly taking the door with them.

"Hey Mum, guess what?"

Therezia was still sitting at the table across from Pietro, both in deep conversation.

The leftovers from lunch were still on the table in front of them indicating that they were too busy talking to notice the passing of time much less the whereabouts of the children.

"Hi kids! You are back early. What is all the excitement about?"

"Mum, remember me telling you about the King Carp?"

"Yes I remember. A nice story. Very inventive."

"No Mum. Not a story. Moya saw it too today."

"Really? Did you really see it Moya?'

Moya did not answer. She was just grinning at Carlos all teeth showing.

Carlos turned around showing her a threatening fist hidden from his mother.

"Yes Mrs Rodriguez, I saw it. It was a very big fish. Nearly as big as I am."

"Really? Did you really see it or just want to back up Carlos's story?"

"No. I would not do that. It was there, a very large fish just cruising slowly on the surface of the water like it owned the place. It probably does, too."

"Okay Carlos. Looks like I'd better start believing your stories, at least some of them."

"Mum, I do not make up stories. Everything I tell you is true. It is not my fault that some of them sound a bit strange."

....

At school, he had no more luck.

No one believed him that he saw again the "King Carp."

And mentioning that he had a witness this time just made things worse for him.

There was open snickering around him.

Going fishing with a girl!

Paul Johnson, the biggest mouth at school started jumping around shouting. "Carlos got a girlfriend! Carlos got a girlfriend!"

He wasn't at it for very long as he got itchy all over suddenly and needed all his attention to concentrate on scratching.

His biology teacher did not do much better.

"Look Carlos, think how this appears to other people. That creek is a very small body of water. Its flow is so slow that it is practically not moving. The murkiness of the water does not let much sunlight in, which means no plant life at the bottom. All this means a very low oxygen level in the water. Fish need more oxygen than that."

"But it is full of fish. We all go fishing there."

"Small fish. The kind of fish you are talking about needs much more oxygen. Although if we are talking about carp, I can't tell you it is impossible. Carps are able to survive in very low oxygen levels. Still it is very improbable."

Carlos was furious standing on the street after school.

They just did not believe him, he was ridiculed by the whole school.

The resentment, the anger was growing inside him.

He felt that he had to hit something or kick something to let some steam off.

"They all called me a liar. I will show them who the liar is."

He concentrated.

Hands tight in fists, a purple light in his eyes............

"Carlos!"

The sharp voice in his mind was like a cold shower, washing

away all the anger, all the resentment.

"Sorry Magda. I nearly......"

"Control, Carlos. Work on it."

"Yes Magda."

....

Pietro became a frequent visitor at Therezia's house and most of the time brought Moya with him.

He had been married before. His wife died in a car accident quite a few years back, so one would expect that he would know how to treat a woman.

This was not so. Pietro behaved like a school boy on his first date, trying to do his best but most of the time things came out upside down.

As for Therezia, in spite of her age, Pietro was her very first suitor so she really did not know how to behave in male company.

When they were together there was always a lot of giggling and embarrassed silences-still even so, they really appeared to enjoy each other's company.

In the meantime, Carlos was getting used to Moya.

He really disliked girls and avoided them as much as he could. He could not comprehend their constant chattering, playing with dolls and all that girlish behaviour.

Moya was different. She did have a big mouth and a loud voice but when she talked she was talking about football or fishing or cars.All boys stuff.

She was good at climbing trees, when she punched Carlos it was a good punch. It hurt and she did not get upset when Carlos punched her back.

If you could ignore her long hair and girlish face she could have passed for a boy.

Carlos liked that.

It also helped that after a while her father stopped forcing her to wear dresses and in pants and a shirt she looked more like a boy.They did a lot of stuff together.

Usually they left the house as it was no fun watching their parent cow eyeing each other.

On the streets they were accepted by the other kids, as the first one that tried to make fun of them, got a punch from Moya.

She was accepted as one of the boys, even sought after when playing soccer as she was quite good at it.

Carlos never liked the "boy stuff"- soccer or any kind of physical activity but with Moya present, he had to force himself. He had to show her what boys really were like.

This meant that he got home exhausted every day but felt much better for it.

If only she weren't a girl.

....

"I think you are not being fair Magda."

"I am trying to be, but I don't believe in coincidences."

"This has nothing to do with me. He is coming to see my mother. Most of the time he ignores me."

"Carlos, you know well that some people are looking for you to do you harm. Anyone turning up suddenly in your life, well, I have to be suspicious of."

"What about Moya?"

"Moya is okay. She is very young and her natural mental defences are not yet developed. I was able to scan her mind. She is fine."

"And Pietro?"

"I do not know. He has very strong mental barriers. I am not sure if they are natural or developed by training."

"Does it matter which one?"

"Of course. If it is natural, like many people have without being aware of it, then it is okay.
But if it has been developed by training, it would mean that he has capacities which he is hiding from us. That would make him dangerous."
"So what are you going to do?"
"Nothing at the moment but I will keep a very close eye on him."
"By the way, I still do not understand why some people want to do me harm. What did I do to them?"
"Your only sin against them was being born."
"Why would that upset them?"
"Carlos, we have talked about this. You know the answer."
"I know. I know. I am not ready to know certain things but that really does not explain anything."
"Your mind at the moment is nearly as unprotected as Moya's. You need a lot of training and growing up to have your barriers in place. As long as your mind is open for anyone to read, you should not have information which is not for everyone to know."
"I hear you. We have talked about this several times. Still, it is a bit frustrating to have to hide from people who want to kill you without knowing who those people are and why they want to harm you."
"I know Carlos, but at the moment I do not have anything better to offer you."

....

At the end of the year school exams were coming up.
Carlos had no problems with that. He was one of the lucky ones, who just had to read something to understand and remember . At least most of the time.
His mind was like a sponge, eager to absorb knowledge.

He wanted to know anything and everything.

Still he wanted to be more and more selective with the data he absorbed.

"I find all this homework business a waste of time"- he complained one day to Magda.

"Do not say that"- was Magda's reply – "You need an education to be a person who counts."

Carlos closed his eyes in concentration and when he opened them, there was a small sparkling diamond in the palm of his hand.

"Would a few of these make a person count?"

"Carlos! Put that carbon back in your pencil!""But Magda..........."

"Carlos! Put it back!"

The sparkling gem disappeared.

""One more act of laziness like this and I will block your mind! You know I can do that."

"I am not lazy."

"Then how do you explain this carbon business?""I just wanted to show you that I do not have to study to be a

rich man."

"Having money in your pocket, would that make you a better man?"

"I could do whatever I wanted to."

"You do not need money for that."

"People would notice me, would consider me an important person."

"Would that make you a better person?"

"Everyone else would think so."

"Would you be a better person?"

"Come on Magda! Don't be difficult. You know what I mean."

"Carlos, I hear you but you cannot possibly mean what you say."

"You are confusing me."

"Carlos, remember, we are connected at many levels of communication. When we talk it's not just words that are passing between us. You cannot possibly lie in a mind link."

"I am not lying."

"Yes you are. You are trying to prove a point to me you yourself do not believe. We have talked about this many times before, and you know perfectly well, that what makes you a person is what is in your head, and not what is in your pocket."

"Okay, okay I agree with you. I need an education and I will study and do my homework, which by the way I have already done."

"I know you have done it."

"And while I do all of that, what is wrong with making some money on the side to help us?"

"There is nothing wrong with making money if you work for it. You can have a newspaper run or do errands like many kids of your age do to make money. But that is not what you were doing."

"I made money."

"Yes, you made money but you did not work for it. You did not deserve that money."

"I don't like to admit it but I think I know what you mean. I felt good when I fixed Moya's dress without her noticing when she tore it fishing. Also I felt bad when I made a kid itchy all over at school just because he upset me."

"Carlos, you are learning. You make me feel that it was worth to spend all this time with you."

"What did I do now?"

"You are growing up. You slowly realise that your power does not make you a big man. What does make you a big man is using this power to help others."

....

Passing the exams was a breeze for Carlos. He did study a lot, regularly did his homework and generally was always doing the right thing.-

He complained about the amount of work he had to do but....deep inside he always knew that he was not being truthful. Because, in spite of all that complaining, he actually enjoyed school stuff. He acquired knowledge he never knew existed. New doors opened for him all over the place, to explore and enjoy.

The mathematical wonders, the magic of chemistry and the ' rules of physics, they were all there to explore and to play with.

With applying his special gifts to the acquired knowledge, the world opened wide around him with fantastic possibilities to explore.

Luckily Moya was around to keep his feet firmly stuck to the ground.

While his mind was chasing the hydrogen atom along its orbit around the oxygen, Moya interrupted saying she needed help to move a piece furniture.

While he was trying to work out the relationship between the urban and the wildlife population, Moya needed help with the shopping.

Moya was always interrupting. Moya was always there molesting.

Moya was part of the furniture.

He missed her when she was not around.

Maybe it was because he was growing up, but by now, the fact that Moya was a girl, was not that bad anymore.

Moya was growing up too.

There were no huge noticeable changes but she was changing slowly. She was still playing soccer with the boys, fishing with Carlos. She still preferred conversations about boy stuff.

Still, she screamed less now during the games and her voice sounded somewhat softer.

Her usual cap disappeared from her head and was replaced by ribbons.

Her shoes were less and less suitable to play soccer in.

Carlos did not notice most of these changes and if he did he did not mind them. What he did start to dislike more and more was the increasing attention the other boys began to give Moya.

And the fact that Moya appeared to enjoy this increased attention.

Carlos himself was surprised by these feelings.

Why should it upset him if Moya smiled at another boy?

Why would it feel so good when Moya picked him out of the group to do something?

These feelings were not logical at all.

Why would the whole afternoon of soccer be spoiled just because she did not turn up?

Why should it be so satisfying when she was watching him kicking a goal?

Carlos was completely confused by these feelings and had no one to talk to about them. His mother was out of the question with this kind of thing. Besides, lately she only had eyes for Pietro.

This was not the kind of subject he could bring up with Magda.

He was on his own and totally confused.

First he tried to avoid Moya but that did not help.

He missed her too much.

Then he tried to be with Moya only when the other boys were not around, this helped for a while, but he could not keep it up forever.

Moya was quite aware of Carlos's mood swings.

At first she really enjoyed the effect she had on Carlos, but noticing how badly he felt about things ,she tried to smooth out the problems.

Once she even held his hand to calm him down. Carlos was surprised about how good that felt.

....

"Magda. Please. I need some help here."

"What is happening? You are supposed to be asleep. Oh I see you got stuck in that box."

"Yes, I got stuck **in** this box.... But how did you know? You can't see it from where you are."

"I am seeing it through your eyes."

"Magda. You know how I feel about that. Besides you promised not to get inside my head."

"Carlos, you called for my help. It sounded urgent. How would I know how to help you?"

"Can you come here?"

"I am here."

The dark figure was sitting on the bed next to Carlos examining his right hand which was half way through the wall of a large metallic box.

Right through the solid wall.

"How the heck did you manage to do this?"

"I was practicing just the way you taught me."

"I have never taught you to do this."

"Well, not quite. I was trying to reach inside the box through the wall."

"Slow down. Give me the details. How did you do it?"

"Okay. First I concentrated on the solid surface of the box trying to visualise the individual particles forming it. The solid wall then expanded and I could see all those small, individual particles which formed it in a very regular, tri dimensional pattern. And relative to the particle's size there were very large empty spaces between them ."

"Good, you visualised the atomic structure of the metal."

"Then I've done the same thing with my hand. The particles were not as regular in alignment but there were still large spaces between the particles."

"I can see where you are going. Keep going"

"So with that many large empty spaces between the particles I thought that I could manipulate my hand's particles along the spaces between the metal particles without them touching."

"Meaning that you reached into the box through its metal wall. So what went wrong?"

"Moya as usual. She was throwing pebbles at my window. She wanted to go and catch rabbits in the forest at night."

"I see. So you lost concentration and your hand's particles got mixed up with the metal atoms."

"Yes. I got stuck."

"Okay. No problem. It is a bit tricky but we can do it. Let me see...."

Magda closed her eyes, concentrating.

After a few minutes there were a few beads of perspiration on her forehead.

"Now, pull your hand out, very slowly."

The hand came out smoothly leaving behind a smooth, unmarked metal surface.

"Thanks Magda. I really thought that I would have to wear that box for the rest of my life."

She did not answer. Magda still had her eyes closed and was breathing deeply and with some difficulty.

"You look exhausted. What's the matter ?"

"That....that separation took a lot of energy. Where do you think it came from?"

"I ......really don't know."

"Every movement, every change requires energy for it to happen. A push bike uses muscle power, a car uses petrol. The changes we are doing also require energy. To make it happen we are using our body's vital energy which is very limited. To remove your hand's particles one by one from amongst the metallic particles required a lot of my body's energy. If you do not mind, I need a bit of a rest before I can go home."

"I did not realise that we had this limitation with what we are able to do."

"It is there alright. I know how to change the moon into green cheese but I do not have the energy to actually do it."

"I do not think anyone has."

"Which is probably a good thing otherwise we would have a big chunk of cheese orbiting the Earth."

•••••••••••••••••••••

"Carlos where are you? Oh, there you are. I have some good
news for you. How would you like to go on a holiday?"
"Mum , we never go on holidays."
"That was mainly because we could not afford it."
"So what is different now?"
"Pietro offered to take all of us to Bali for a week. How do you
feel about it?"
"I heard a lot of nice things about Bali but you have to fly to
get there."
"Well, that or a very long swim. What is wrong about flying?"
"Nothing. I just don't like the idea."
"You are not afraid of flying? You had no problem with boats."
"That is because if something goes wrong I can swim. I can't
fly."
"Come on. Nothing can go wrong with a plane."
"Then why are they crashing all over the world?"
"They are not crashing all over the world. Sometimes
accidents happen. That is all. It will not happen to us."
"You promise?"
"I do. So what about putting on a happy face and say you
would love to go to Bali."
"I would love to go to Bali. By the way who is going?"
"All four of us."
"Sounds like a family group."
"It does, doesn't it?"
"And when are we supposed to go? What about school?"
"No excuse there, smart Alek. School is finishing in three
weeks and we are going after that."
....

"I am not happy about this flying business Magda.""Carlos, fear is a very unproductive feeling."

"I know that but I have no control over how I feel about things."

"No one has control over that, but how you react to it, well, that is entirely up to you."

"So what do I do?"

"Instead of accepting fear as a fact look for a solution."

"What solution do you have for the fear of flying?"

"The fear is not about flying. The fear is about falling when you are flying. If you can make sure that you cannot fall, there would be no reason left to fear."

"And how can I do that?"

"Okay. Let's Imagine the situation, now that you are safely on the ground.

You are in the plane, suddenly, the engines fail and the plane is starting to fall. What can you personally do?"

"Well, I could change water molecules in the air to hydrogen under the plane."

"Yes. Have a cushion of hydrogen to hold up the plane. It could work. Especially next to the red hot engines."

"Ouch! I would blow up the plane."

"Anything else?"

"Well I could change the gravity around the plane."

"Could you do that?"

"No."

"So why bring it up? Anything else?"

"No other ideas. I guess I would crash with the plane."

"Unless you could find a few friends who could help you out in a situation like that."

"And where would I..... Oh sorry Magda. I know you would look after me."

"Of course I would and a lot of others too. You have met most of them during your training sessions."

"You are the only one I've I met face to face." "You will meet them when the time is right. In the meanwhile, what about that fear of flying?"

"What fear of flying? Knowing that you are kind of holding my hand all the way I will feel safer than in my bed at home."

....

There was no fear of flying on the plane. Partly because Carlos was too busy fighting with Moya for a turn at the window seat.

For both of them this was the first travelling experience and they spent most of their time with their noses stuck to the window, although all they could see were clouds.

Still, the changing shapes of the cloud formations gave plenty for a child's imagination.

They competed in who could see the strangest, most bizarre shapes in the hazy, white formations.

On arrival new surprises were awaiting them.

First it was the heat.

The weather in Bali is expected to be warm but this was an unusually hot day.

When they stepped out of the air-conditioned plane, at the top of the stairs, and began to walk down them to the ground, it was like a blast of heat in their face and by the time they got to the bottom of the stairs they were all soaked in perspiration.

They did not really mind the heat. The newness of the situation just produced more excitement and expectation of what was to come.

And there were plenty of things coming.

Carlos had never seen coloured people before and here they

were everywhere.

The colours, the smells, the new visual challenges, it was the first time ever that they were both quiet for a long time.

The bus drive to their hotel was very disappointing for them as it was too short. Not long enough to soak up much of the local colour.

The hotel itself was also full of new things to explore. The tropical themes, palm trees and green stuff everywhere. And all those smiling people around showing their white teeth and their dark skins, highlighted even more by the brightly coloured clothes they wore.

Especially the women, flowing dresses, flowers in their hair, bright colours everywhere.

The adults were impressed too but for the children all this had a magical quality. So different from their usual environment that it was difficult to accept all this as reality.

Therezia and Pietro decided to have a rest and got themselves comfortable in one of the open areas with a drink in their hands. Giving the children the perfect opportunity to disappear.

Carlos wanted to sit down at the entrance and observe the lazy way things were happening. Just watching the world go by, people milling around; but this was not good enough for Moya.

Almost forcibly, she dragged Carlos around with her, exploring every possible place reachable on foot.

The hotel was quite away from the business part of the town but there were lots of things happening all around.

The building inside was full of statues, carved wood columns and dark mysterious places but the real activity was outside, along the beach line.

There were quite a lot of people swimming, kayaking or

snorkelling but Carlos noted that all that frenzied activity was done only by the white people, the tourists.

The locals, always smiling, were walking around at a more sedate, laid back pace.

There were a lot of little tent shops along the water selling all sorts of souvenirs. Luckily they had no money or they would have bought everything.

All those wood carvings and things made of shell looked so exotic.

They wanted it all.

The water looked very inviting too but they were told not to get in the water without the adults being present.

Maybe it was the strangeness of the situation but perhaps for the first time they actually did what they were told.

The rest of the day passed very fast for everyone and by the night time, both adults and children were exhausted.

They had two rooms. Therezia and Moya slept in one of them and Pietro and Carlos in the other. Not one of them was happy with this arrangement but Pietro felt it was the correct thing to do.

The next day was very busy. They decided that as they probably would not return to Bali again, they would see and do everything possible during the week.

They started in the market where rows after rows of small tent like structures were offering their wares. One could buy anything. Shoes, clothes, handbags, and souvenirs, whatever one wanted. They were warned about the prices and told not to look for any 'quality' items, still, it was difficult not to get interested in the myriad of exotic items offered.

While the girls were looking for dresses and Pietro for souvenirs, Carlos was looking around the wood carvings.

There were thousands of them in just about every little shop.

All strangely shaped gods and goddesses, dogs and winged
beasts.
All shiny and new, but Carlos was not looking for those.
He was searching for something unique, one of a kind, old
and really exotic.
After a while he found what he wanted.
Under one of the tables, holding up one of it's a wobbly legs,
was a dirty, black statue.
It was the usual sacred bird carrying a god on its back, while
itself standing on the back of a turtle representing the world
with the serpent of life coiling all around it.
It was dirty, cracked in the middle but under the dirt he could
see the glint of the original gold painting. It looked very old.
He got it very cheap as nobody appeared to want it.
The vendor looked oddly at the young tourist who wanted to
buy rubbish instead of the shiny carvings, but Carlos was very
happy with his find. With a bit of cleaning and repairing this
statue would look absolutely fantastic.
After the market they went to the temple of the monkeys.
They were warned about the inquisitive nature of the animals,
still it was hard to keep those agile hands out of their
pockets or bags.
One of them managed to get hold of Therezia's sunglasses,
the ones she had just bought at the market and retired with it
to one of the trees. It just stayed there examining it no matterhow
much fuss Therezia made.The other tourists just laughed as realistically
there was
nothing anyone could have done.
Except Carlos.
He grabbed Therezia's hand to calm her down.
"Do not scream at him. Ask nicely. They are trained monkeys,
used to people. He probably will bring it back if you look

friendly."

Therezia was too upset to be able to do it, so Carlos approached the tree and extended his empty hand to the animal.

"Please monkey, we need those glasses. Bring it back to me, please."

No one saw the purple light in his eyes.

The monkey stopped playing with the glasses and looked at Carlos for a long time.

After a while, very slowly, as though unsure of what he was doing, the monkey came down from the tree and gave Carlos the sunglasses.

Then, as if he awoke with the loud cheering of the people around, jumped back up to the tree and disappeared amongst its branches.

Lunch was a bit of a waste of time as they had to go back to the hotel for it. Everywhere they went there were shops offering all kind of exotic food, but they were warned about eating anything bought on the street in Bali. The dreaded "Bali Belly", caused by infected water, was a very nasty disease which could really spoil everyone's holiday. It did not affect the natives as they were used to the bugs but the tourists were not. Some of them had a really bad time.

After lunch, it was the beach.

While Pietro and Therezia lay lazily on the sand under a long beach umbrella, Moya and Carlos took to the water.

They got some snorkelling gear from the hotel and decided to see what was there under the water.

It was very disappointing.

They both expected to see beautiful corals, colourful fish, just like on the postcards but there was nothing much to see. The sea was nice and warm and so clear that one could see quite a distance under the water.

They were on a long, sandy beach, with no rocks or plants or anything along the long, parallel ripples of the nearly white sandy bottom. A few dead shells here and there, some small crabs burrowing themselves under the sand and a few green/grey fish flashing through.

That was all.

They swam to the far end of the beach where a few large rocks were sticking out of the water as an extension of the small cliff on land.

Here, the picture changed.

The water around the rocks teamed with life.

There were large green patches of plants on the rocks and on the rocky bottom. Together with long branches of pink and brown soft coral feeding in the warm water. Star fish of all colours, Even some large blue, red and yellow anemones stretching their fleshy arms to reach for food; as well as a few groups of purple hard coral growing on the rocks.

And the fish.

Hundreds of them. Thousands.

Every imaginable colour and shape darted amongst the branches of the sea fans and feather stars.

This small, localised area of the beach looked more alive, more colourful even than the postcards they saw.

They even glimpsed a turtle going by but could not get close enough to it.

It was just too fast.

Both of them stayed in the water until their bellies began protesting in hunger. When they finally got out, their skin was white and wrinkled due to the long stay in the water.

And every day passed just like that.

In the morning, it was the mad rush around to see all the

sights, the shops, the temples, which by the way, were everywhere.

Every day brought something new, something interesting.

One morning they bought a nice painting in one of the shops. The friendly owner invited them to see his private collection of paintings.

He had a lot of nice ones , most of them abstracts or typical Balinese story paintings. But he had one hanging there on the wall which was quite different.

It was a classic painting of a Madonna and child, both with a halo around their heads.

It was a very old painting. The paint was chipped and lifting in several parts, curling up, separating from the canvas.

The shopkeeper very proudly declared that a few years back his father had an exhibition of his paintings in one of the museums in Sydney, Australia, and when he was packing up to come home, he "accidently" packed away this painting too. The local heat and the moisture in the air were really ruining that old masterpiece.

....

A few days later they had a practical demonstration of the quality of the water in Bali. They stopped at a river crossing to observe the local people go about their businesses.

It was a wide, slow moving river, and along the banks, there were groups of women washing clothes , bare to the waist, and carrying the wicker baskets with the clothes on top of their heads.

Among them, here and there, were people washing themselves standing in knee deep water, with groups of children playing noisily in the water.

Right in the middle of all this, an old man was emptying his bowels in the shallow water. No one seemed particularly upset about it. It appeared to be the natural thing to do.

....

The adults spent the afternoon lazing on the beach or around the pool recovering the energy spent during the morning, so the children were free to do whatever they wanted.

They explored every part of the hotel, inside and out.

In the kitchen the cooks gave them special treats, the cleaners showed them ways to get to the dark, hidden places not frequented by tourists.

The gardener showed them his "special" plants, the ones he was growing in a distant corner of the hotel garden, away from the eyes of most of the other guests.

They were asked not to mention them to anyone.

One afternoon, one of the local fishermen on the beach showed them his "special spot" to catch fish.

There was a very large rock with a flat top standing half in and half out of the water. On the outside edge of the rock, the water was quite deep and a lot of people tried their luck there but no one seemed to catch a decent fish.

What they did not know – as the fisherman explained to Carlos and Moya – was that under the water there were large caves and a lot of large fish rested there during the day.

There were small holes on the top of the rock which no one noticed because they looked like small puddles, but they went down into the underwater caverns.

So while all the others were standing at the edge of the rock throwing their lines far into the blue water, this fellow was standing a few metres behind them on the flat rock, letting his line down into one of the small holes.

In just a few minutes he caught two nice fish while the others had nothing.

....

The children's afternoons were busier than the mornings
and when they had nothing special to explore , they spent the
time in the water enjoying the colourful marine life.
However, there was one thing they did not notice.
Whatever Carlos and Moya did, they were doing it together.
They ate together, they played together, and they went
everywhere together.
One never went anywhere without the other.
This was not planned, it just happened.
They were a team.

....

"But I did think about your Magda!"
"Carlos, when will you learn not to lie in a mind link?"
"But I did think about you – sometimes."
"You were on holiday. You were not supposed to think about
me or school or anything else.
But holidaying is over so what about starting to work again?
You were not very good on those fire control exercises."
"Okay, okay I will practice."

....

The holiday was nice, beautiful, enjoyable, all of that and
more, but it was over. School started too, which occupied
most of his days, quite uselessly in Carlos's opinion.
He did not like school at all.
He still had this need, this push inside to acquire more
knowledge but he found that he could learn more and do it
faster in the library by himself.
School was much too slow for him.
And when he was given a computer with internet access for
his birthday, even the library became obsolete.

....

Carlos was trying all sorts of excuses to miss school. His main argument was that if school was there to give him an education then he did not need school as he could manage his education much better and much faster by himself.

Pietro tried explaining to him again and again that having an education was not enough. To get anywhere in this society one needed that piece of paper to prove that they had that education.

To get that piece of paper he had to go to school.

Carlos did not like it but he accepted the idea.

He was studying hard every day but not quite what the teachers wanted him to study. This of course explained the fact that his grades were good but never very good.

He also practiced part of the night under Magda's and the other's supervision.

Therezia had learned for a long time now, to ignore the smells and noises coming from his room.

It was lucky that he needed very little sleep in order to be bright and fresh by the morning.

His social life on the other hand, was not very successful.

At school, probably because he was far younger than the other pupils, Carlos did not have any close friends; he just could not share their interests.

In the neighbourhood he shared activities with children of his own age, but even with them, he had no shared interests

His learning, especially the night practices, put him in a group of his own.

Moya was the only person of his age he could feel close to.

By this time, Moya's being a girl stopped being an issue, and she was accepted as equal in everything. She behaved and was accepted as a boy, not just by Carlos, but by the other kids also.

And if one of them did not accept her, he learned fast after a punch on the nose.

....

"Hi Magda. Sorry for calling you but something strange happened today."

"Tell me about it."

"I was coming home from school, walking through the shopping centre when my ring, the snake ring, the one you gave me, got very tight on my finger. It was so tight that it was nearly painful. It lasted only a few minutes, then stopped."

"Was anyone close to you? Did you talk to anyone?"

"I did not talk to anyone but there were a lot of people around."

"Did you notice anything unusual? Like someone watching you?"

"No. there was just people around, all minding their own business. What does it mean? It has never happened before."

"If anything like this happens again please call me straight away. No matter where you are."

"Okay, but what does it mean?"

"Remember when I told you that some people are looking for you to do you harm? Well the tightening of the ring is a warning that one of them is close by. When this happens, get away from there, fast, but be careful not to call attention on yourself. The tightening of the ring means that they are physically close but their attention is not directed toward you, so you are safe."

"So they were looking for me but did not find me?"

"Possibly, but most likely they just passed by and their proximity was purely accidental."

"How do I know when they find me?"

"When one of those people's attentions is directed towards you the ring does not just become tight, the snake lifts its head and hisses."

"That is neat. And don't you worry, I can defend myself."

"I suggest you do nothing but call me. Nothing else. By doing something you would just confirm your identity. Besides it is hard to identify the person. They could be absolutely anyone you might see around you."

"So I just call you and run?"

"Call me but do not run. That just would call attention to you."

"I still don't understand why these people are looking for me."

"Carlos, we have talked about this. Please trust me on this, without asking for the reason. You will know everything soon enough"

"Magda, I have always accepted your advice. Still I have a question about the ring. It is a very visual and unusual ring but no one seems to notice it. I was flashing it all around but no one even commented or asked questions about it. Not even Moya and she's got a big mouth.""Carlos, no one else can see that ring except our kind. So if

anyone does make a comment about your ring, you'll know what kind of person they are."

"Our kind? You have never used this term before. What is our kind?"

"People who have an unusual capacity, who can do things most others cannot do.

People who have to hide or at least hide their capacity in order to be able to live in this society. That is what I mean by our kind. We are different but we do everything possible to hide this difference."

"It does not sound very fair."

"It is not, but in any aspect of life people who cannot do something, resent the ones who can. This would apply to sports, business, artistic capacity or anything else.""And if the majority can't do that thing, the ones who can are

in trouble. The more different they are, the bigger the trouble."

"Correct. So to avoid trouble, they hide."

"And no one tried to fight back?"

"How do you fight? How do you change public opinion?"

"By showing the people that we could be useful. That it is a good idea having us around."

"It has been tried many times and always led to disaster. People do not like to feel inferior.

Still, I am happy that you did not choose the other alternative."

"Which is?"

"Brute force."

"Well, if we organise ourselves, we could be stronger than everyone else combined."

"True, but fear can produce far more enemies than a feeling of inferiority"

"We could still dominate."

"True. Then what?"

"What do you mean then what?"

"Well, you have now dominated the world by force. Can you run it?"

"What do you mean run it?"

"Well, you've taken over from every leader, every large organisation that has been managing things up till now. Can you perform all of their functions on your own?"

"Why would I have to take over?"

"Because you started a war. Every leader, every group you leave free will turn against you."

"I don't think that there is enough of us to do that. To manage the world."

"Well, then you have only two alternatives. To kill everyone or to enslave everyone. Which one do you fancy?"

"I do not fancy any of your choices. I think I will keep hiding. At least until there are enough of us to emerge as equals."

"Carlos, you don't know just how very important it is for you to feel like that."

....

For Carlos's 10th birthday Therezia wanted to organise a big party. She wanted to invite all his friends, which caused a bit of a problem.

He did not really have any friends.

So Therezia invited kids from the neighbourhood, kids Carlos used to play with.

At the end there were about fourteen kids present together with some of the parents who were mostly Therezia's friends.

There was plenty of food and organised activities but as usual, a party organised by adults for kids was a bit of a flop.

Carlos saved the party spirit by performing some magic tricks that amazed both kids and adults.

Everyone wanted to know how he changed the colours of the balls just by covering them with a cloth which itself changed colours.

Or the green frogs which were jumping out of his empty hands into a box, which was in turn completely empty afterwards.

Carlos did not explain anything, saying that a magician is not allowed to reveal his secrets.

And one of the mothers was good with balloon animals, which was also fun.

Still, the biggest success was the dance one of the boys performed after Moya kicked him under the table for calling her names.

So the party was a success as far as everyone was concerned.

Except for Therezia.

The main reason she organised this party was to get Carlos some friends. She was really upset seeing him alone most of the time.

Carlos was friendly with everyone; lots of kids were seeking his company. He played soccer, went swimming in the creek with them, was invited frequently to their places, still there was no one he could really call a friend.

At school all the kids were three or four years older than him, which at his age was very significant.

They shared very little common interests.

The neighbourhood kids of his own age, maybe because of his intense studying with Magda, he found mostly very childlike. He accepted their invitations but did not seek their company.

Except Moya's.

Moya was different.

She was loud, she was irritating. She was always doing something unexpected and she always managed to upset him.

She was absolutely a pain in the neck and Carlos had many times decided not to see her any more.

These decisions never lasted long as he very soon began to miss her company.

Moya was Moya and she was the only person Carlos felt comfortable with, even the times when he really hated her for the things she did.

Moya knew all this and really enjoyed upsetting him but then one word, a smile or a touch of her hand was enough to calm him down.

Pietro was a constant part of their lives now as he appeared to get along with Therezia very well.

Magda was not very happy about this. She could not find out anything about him, good or bad, and for some reason she was not able to trust him.

Naturally there was nothing she could actually do about the situation.

Carlos liked Pietro. He was quiet, soft talking and always nice to him but there was no special bond between them. He could not accept Pietro as part of the family as Therezia did.

For him Pietro was always a nice visiting stranger.

Carlos was trying to read him as he was able to do with many of the kids, but Pietro appeared to have a formidable mental barrier. Except for a few surface thoughts Carlos could not pick up anything from him.

Maybe it was due to Magda's influence but he did not really feel close to him.

He also met another of his night teachers, Steven.

Carlos was sitting in the park talking to Magda when Steven arrived. He was wearing the same ring as Carlos and when they shook hands the snakes lifted their heads but did not hiss at each other.

At first impression, Steven appeared to be a very old man .

His hair was very white, his face and hands thin and much wrinkled. The second glance, however, denied this age as he stood very straight and moved with the agility of a young man. He carried a walking stick, perhaps more as an ornament as he was not using it as a walking aid.

Carlos really liked that walking stick. It had a large silver lion's head as a handle with red crystal eyes which appeared to be alive.

Steven had a very soft, deep voice and unusual purplish blue eyes.

Carlos had always liked the nightly contacts with him and now he found a very nice physical person also.

Steven was a teacher at the local school, teaching older boys. It would be a few years before Carlos would get to be in his class.

There was no special reason for this meeting except that Magda wanted Carlos to begin slowly to meet all of his teachers, then later the rest of their group of "special people". What Magda wanted was for Carlos to eventually become an active part of their community.

Carlos was happy with the idea that now he had two people to call on if he ever needed help.

....

"What do you think about Pietro, Carlos?"

"He is a nice man, Mum. I like him."

"How would you like to live in the same house with him?"

"I don't know Mum. I have never thought about that. Why do you ask?"

"I like Pietro very much and he appears to like me. We get along well together. Yesterday he asked me to marry him."

"And what did you say?"

"I said I needed time to think it over"

"What do you want time for? Either you want him or you don't."

"I want him. I just wanted to talk it over with you first."

"What do I have to do with this?"

"Carlos, Pietro became very important in my life, but still he is just number two. You will always be the number one in my life. I do not want to do anything which would cause you discomfort."

"Mum, I love you too. If you feel Pietro is the man for you, don't let him go. I do not know much about him, but he appears to be a nice man and I have no problem with the idea of living in the same house with him."

"Carlos, I love you. You are a good son."

"But where would we all live? His house is quite small and his one isn't big enough either."

"We were thinking about selling both houses and buying a bigger one."

"Mum, I hope you can pull it off, but neither of our houses has much value."

"Yes, that is a problem. We have already made enquiries, and in today's market our houses are both very low in value. We were looking for an affordable house but for now we have not found one."

"So what are you going to do?"

"I am not sure. We cannot get married if we can't afford to live together."

"So you just wait?"

"Well, we are not getting any younger, but what else can we do? We just have to find an affordable place to live in."

....

"Steven, I need your advice."

"Talk to me."

"I've got problems with my mother. For the first time there is a good man in her life, but they can't get married because they can't afford to buy a larger house where we could all live together."

"So what do you think you should do about it?"

"I do not know. That is why I need your advice. I've got several ways to make money but last time I made a diamond, Magda got very upset about it."

"Now hold on! I know about that and it was an entirely different thing. You used your talent to create wealth you did not need, did not work for, and did not deserve."

"Magda said exactly the same thing, and made me undo the diamond. This deserving business, how do I know when and what someone deserves?"

"What you deserve in life is very hard to explain in words. It is more like a gut feeling thing. It depends on many things. What sort of person we are talking about, what are the present circumstances, what are this person's needs, what were this persons actions to fulfil this need.

Let's go back to your diamond. Do you really believe that you should have had it? That you deserved it?"

"Well.....no."

"Now think about your mother. Does she deserve a gift of money to buy a new house?"

"She definitely deserves it. She has worked hard all her life, sacrificing everything for Sarah and me. For the first time she has the opportunity to have a happy, normal life and she can't afford it. I really think that she needs that money. She worked for it and deserves it."

"So what do you want me for? You have your answer"

"Okay, cleared this, thank you. Now what do I do? Make another diamond?"

"No, nothing like that. First you would find it very hard to convert it to money and second, how would you explain where you got it?"

"What else could I do?"

"Well let's thinks about it. Let's imagine that a very rich person is travelling with a large group of friends, servants and a spoiled cat. When they go through these parts the cat disappears. There is a very large amount of money offered as a reward to whomever recovers the cat, partly because it is a loved pet, partly because it is wearing a very expensive diamond collar which is naturally not advertised."

"And I find the cat. Can you arrange all this?"
"I do not need to arrange anything. I just have to advertise the reward in the paper then get a cat for you to find."
....
Everyone liked the new house.
it was next to a small lake with very few houses around.
With empty blocks at both sides which gave them plenty of privacy.
The large garden kept Therezia in constant excitement as she had always dreamed of working in her own garden but has never had the chance.
The house itself was unusually large, for all of them.
They were all used to small, cramped places and the open, large spaces of the house were strange to get used to.
Sometimes it was a problem finding each other along the long corridors and large rooms.
The bedrooms were all upstairs together with two bathrooms.
Moya's bedroom was close to the adult's bedroom but Carlos's room was nearly on the other end of the house.
He was quite happy with this arrangement as he worried about the noises caused by his nightly activities, and his room had a small balcony, which was perfect for the smelly stuff.
Carlos insisted on having a lock on his room, as he wanted to prevent Moya's unexpected visits.
Their school was a bit further away, but Pietro could drive them there in the morning and pick them up in the afternoon.
As there were very few houses in the area there were not many kids in the neighbourhood what Carlos did not really mind. He spent most of his time with his nose in books, although most of them were not the ones recommended by his school teachers.
Magda and Steven taught him how to do a lot of new things

but their scant explanation about why things happened the way they did, was not very satisfying.

He wanted to know more, much more.

More details.

He wanted to understand the inner workings of metallic objects, what made them what they were, the forces that maintained, changed and manipulated them.

Sometimes he had problems obtaining the books he wanted from the library as the librarians could not understand what a ten year old boy wanted with books many adults would not understand.

It was easier to obtain information from the internet, but Carlos found that it was difficult to assess the trustworthiness of the data obtained. Anyone could place things on the internet and Carlos indeed found a lot of false information there.

Luckily the end of the school year was approaching again and Moya was busy with her own studies, causing less of a disturbance in Carlos's life.

His school situation did not really change. Carlos passed all his exams but not with flying colours as he did not study much for them.

Probably due to Magda's influence, his general maturity reached and perhaps passed the level of his older school mates. Still, he found no friends amongst them.

While their interest turned more and more to girls and having fun, Carlos had his nose stuck in the books piled up in his room wherever there was still an empty place.

The expression of having stuck his nose up to the sky naturally came from Moya who was quite often upset by Carlos's sitting motionless, sometimes for hours on end, looking at a fixed point and being unresponsive to her.

Moya liked action, movement, and was bored on her own.

At the same time Carlos needed these quiet, thinking periods. In his mind he had to bring together and balance two worlds. His everyday world with his family, school and normal childhood which, by the way, was passing very fast, and the world in which during the night he learned and absorbed the information provided by his night teachers.

The two worlds were very different, even opposite in some concepts and uniting them together in one mind, in one life, was quite a task.

Magda recognised when this task became too heavy and left him long, free periods to organise his mind, to cope with the differences in life concepts.

Moya did not really understand what was going on but accepted his mood changes and learned when to leave him alone.

Their parents of course had no idea of what was going on. Pietro appeared to notice these mood changes but did not make any comments.

CHAPTER THREE

On the way home from the library Carlos was deep in thought.

Things just did not want to make any sense.

If particles of the same charge repelled each other, then how come the particles of solid things stayed together?

The closer the particles were to each other the more solid the object was.

They even appeared to attract each other. The closer they were the bigger this attraction was.

The same particles. They should reject each other.

But then, if the particles would reject each other and the distance in between the particles were getting larger and larger, then no solid objects would exist.

Everything would be in a gaseous form.

Obviously this didn't happen, but why not?

It did not make any sense.

"Hey boy – watch where you are going!"

The strong hand grabbing his shoulder pulled him back before he stepped down from the footpath- without looking.

"Thank you... sorry.... I was not looking."

"Better watch out. You nearly stopped in front of the bus."

The tall, well dressed older man was smiling at him but his strong, claw like fingers did not let his shoulder go.

As if waking up Carlos just realised that his ring was quite tight around his finger and now the head of the snake was lifting up and hissing at the man.

"It looks like your ring does not like me...."

"How can you see it?"

"Well, I got a similar ring and it does not like you either. Look at him hissing at you."

A bit too late Carlos realised what was happening and in a

panic closed his fist pressing hard on the ring.

"Thank you for holding me back. I must go now. My mother is expecting me."

"Come on kid, you can be a lot more thankful for my saving you. Just come with me for a minute. I want to show you something."

"Hello Zacharias.""

"Ahhh... hello Magda! And hello to you too Steven! Little boy, you have some very powerful guardians."

"Zacharias. What are you doing this way?"

"Well, I just happened to pass through on my way."

"And you just happened to bump into Carlos?"

"Yes and he is lucky that I did. He was just about to get hit by a bus."

"I think he is safe now. You can let him go."

"Well, he is a nice boy. I just wanted to talk to him."

"Zacharias! You do not really want to upset me. Or do you?"

"No one in his sane mind would want to upset you Magda. Still, you cannot do anything to me. You know the rules."

"Unless you release him right now...."

"Okay little boy. It looks like your guardians want you. Better go with them."

With a marked reluctance the old man released his hold on Carlos's shoulder, then turning around, he disappeared in the traffic.

"How do you feel Carlos?"

"I am fine. But I am not sure about what happened here just now."

"What exactly do you remember?"

"That you were quite rude to a nice old man."

"That nice old man was just about to kidnap you."

"That nice old man probably saved my life by not letting the bus hit me."

"Carlos, how well do you know this street?"

"I've been on this street ever since I could walk."

"And how many times did you see a bus here?"

"Every day,..............no...that is not right. The bus never comes this way. That sneaky old man made me see the bus. He was controlling me."

"Correct, and in a few minutes you would have gone happily with him to never see daylight again."

"But why? Why would he want to do this to me?"

"Steven, what do you think?"

Steven just shrugged his shoulders.

"I think it is time to talk to him, Magda."

"It appears to be so. I expected to have this conversation a few years later, but Zacharias's appearance changes things. Okay Carlos, let's sit down in that park around the corner and talk."

The park was large, full of trees and quiet. In the middle of the week not many people had time to walk around here.

As they sat down on a long bench in the shade, Carlos was not sure about the subject of their conversation but felt the seriousness in the air and kept quiet.

Magda was very serious too.

"Carlos you remember we talked many times about the interaction of normal people and people with special talents. That we have to hide our talents in order to live in peace together. I have told you many times the problems it could cause if we came out in the open. Remember how many times I told you not let people know what you are able to do?"

"I remember."

"Good. People like us, we are very much in the minority. Humans are funny animals, they do not tolerate having someone who is different amongst them. Especially if they are afraid of him."

"We are stronger than them, we could defend ourselves."

"Maybe yes, but we are very few in number, and even if we could win the war, which would be inevitable, the casualties on both sides would be horrific." "So we avoid confrontation, try to live in peace, at least until we become the majority. Then we would be the normal."

"Correct. This is exactly what I am trying to teach you and expect you to live by."

"So where does Zacharias come into this story?"

"Well the problem is that not everyone agrees to accept the things the way they are. There is a division within our kind. Some of our people believe that it is time to show our colours, by force, if necessary"

"You mean that they want to eliminate the normal human race?"

"Well, I am sure they had considered that possibility but it is not a functional solution. They need people to run the country, to work in the factories, on the land. Without the normal populace, the world would collapse."

"Then they have to plan to enslave them."

"Not quite. If they could infiltrate the government, the military, the key environmental positions, they could do anything they want, legally."

"And where do I and Zacharias come into it?"

"They go around collecting all the young people, to bring them up and educating them to follow their way."

"It is a very nasty thing to do."

"Not quite, it is very practical. We do the same thing."

"And where do I come in? Remember that nasty dog business? They didn't try to educate me. They were trying to kill me."

"You are different. You have special, quite unique talents. They know that you could grow up being a very powerful person under proper guidance. They know that you could be a very powerful leader on our side and they don't want that."

"So that is why you are cramming into my head the life of all those world leaders. How they lived, what they did right and what did they did wrong. You want me to be that mystical leader."

"I do not choose for you what you will be or not. I am just trying to give you the capacity to be what you choose to be."

....

Life went on.

For weeks, then months, nothing happened.

Carlos went to school, fought with Moya nearly every day for something silly. Therezia was happy as a school girl with Pietro – everything appeared normal.

On the outside.

On the inside, though, Carlos changed a lot.

The meeting with Zacharias left its mark.

Carlos at eleven was too young to understand the meaning of that meeting in a global sense but at the same time he was old enough to understand being attacked by an enemy, the hurt and the pain.He also did understand that he was in a situation of constant danger from powerful enemies and decided to do something about it.

Although the concept of why he was in danger was still not very clear to him, Magda appeared to take it very seriously and whatever Magda thought about something, it was always correct. ....

At a very early stage in his life Magda was teaching him how to open his mind and receive thoughts from the outside to facilitate his night training from a distance.

Later on this became a bit of a problem as Carlos started to receive unwanted thoughts and emotions from people around him.

To correct this Magda showed him how to put up a mental barrier in order to selectively keep out unwanted emotions.

Carlos still had chills running up his back when thinking about how easily Zacharias had controlled him.

That could not happen again.

He practiced very hard with Magda and Steven to build up a mental barrier to keep out people from his mind.

This was, with a lot of work, finally achieved and eventually not even Magda could penetrate his mental barrier, no matter how hard she tried.

The real problem was not to form this barrier but how to maintain it, as it cost him quite an effort to keep it up even for a few minutes.

It took him many months of hard work to strengthen this barrier to remain functional for a longer period and quite a few years to achieve a permanent mind barrier.

But protecting his mind's integrity was not enough.

He had to be able to get out of dangerous situations.Many times during the day he imagined threatening situations,

then worked out how to get safely out of them.

Like if suddenly the ground would open up under him and he fell into a deep hole.

He would simply change part of the solid wall into a gaseous form and just allow the expanding air to push him out of the hole.

Or like when turning around a corner he suddenly finds

himself face to face with a charging bull.He would just expand the body mass of the bull into small

particles which would just pass around him then reassemble into the bull again behind him.

He imagined meeting Zacharias again.

While holding his screen very tight, he loosened by vibration a brick on the building above his head...

By separating the particles forming the ground under his feet he created a deep hole...

By increasing the movements of the air particles around his body he created intense heat, burning him to cinders...

Carlos really did not like Zacharias.

He was really angry about the easy way Zacharias had controlled him and his not even being aware of it.

Carlos concentrated his anger in creating in his mind again and again methods how to destroy Zacharias.

His anger made his practicing more intense, but at the same time, harder to control.

Magda always told him to concentrate in calmness before engaging in any mental work. Carlos understood that calmness and concentration were important but with Zacharias this just did not work. There was too much anger and resentment involved.

So Carlos was really busy.

School work during the day, training at night with Magda and Steven and doing his "war preparation" during any free moment.

Realistically, Carlos did not mind this.

Except for his school work, which he still declared useless but something he had to do. He really enjoyed his mental training. After all this time it felt to him more natural than learning from books.

Therezia did not understand what was happening but welcomed this sudden seriousness of Carlos. She took it as a sign of burgeoning maturity arriving.

The only person who did not like this mood change was Moya who missed their playing and fighting times.

She tried to approach him time and again but Carlos more often than not got upset with the interruption.

After a while, Moya gave up and surprisingly, left him alone, which in turn irritated Carlos who had become used to, and missed her interruptions.

....

It was hot.

It was after lunch.

The class was absolutely boring.

Carlos had to put all of his attention in the effort of not falling asleep.

In the somnolent heat Mrs Barna's monotonous voice had a hypnotic quality.

At least half the class was nearly asleep.

Mrs Barna, however, did not notice any of this. With her back towards the students she was concentrating on the shape of the flower she was drawing on the blackboard, while pointing out and describing the different parts of its botanical anatomy. She was quite convinced that such a fascinating subject would have all her students sitting on the edge of their seats, wondering about the miraculous creation of nature she was describing.

Carlos was really trying to concentrate, fixing his eyes on the back of Mrs Barna's admirable figure. Her figure was admirable in her width as she was covering nearly half of the blackboard.

It was just impossible to concentrate on what she was saying.

His mind was not able to follow the meaning of that slow, somnolent voice which was the expression of Mrs Barna's excitement about the subject.

During the last few weeks Magda was trying to teach him about out of body experiences with very little success. He was just unable to follow her instructions about how to leave his own body behind.

He was stuck to it too much.

Carlos felt very uneasy about the idea of getting out of his body and just leaving it behind.

He failed every time he tried, upsetting Magda, who kept saying that he had the capability but was just afraid to let go.

Today was quite different, though.

There was nothing tying him down to this place.

With every fibre of his body he wanted to get away.

Maybe if he tried now.

Mrs Barna was unlikely to turn around for a long while and the other students were not giving him any attention.

So he tried.

Just the way Magda had told him to before.

To imagine the feeling that his body was around him, encasing him.

He was inside, trying to climb out.

Slowly forcing himself through a small opening on the top of his head, leaving behind an empty shell.

The progress was slow, requiring a lot of effort.

Quite frightening but at the same time exhilarating.

Then with a "pop"- he was out.

It was a strange but absolutely wonderful feeling.

He felt free, completely, unusually free.

No weight, just this wonderful, floating feeling.

He could stretch in every direction without any limits.

Watching his body sitting down there amongst his half asleep school mates with Mrs Barna still facing the blackboard.
Carlos looked up and he could see the sky through the ceiling of the room.
He could float towards the sky through the ceiling of the room Higher and higher. The sun bathed him but he could not feel the heat.
The clouds were moving fast but he could not feel the wind.
He was soaring higher and higher following the clouds.....
Mrs Barna's ruler came down on the desk in front of him making a very sharp noise.
"Mr Rodriguez, are you with us?"
Carlos was suddenly aware of her angry face on top of her voluminous body.
He was also aware of the snickering classmates, quite happy that the teacher's attention was now on someone else.
At the same time he was still soaring amongst the clouds.
"Mr Rodriguez?"
Carlos was unable to answer, unable to move.
He was aware of the emptiness of his body and was desperately trying to get back inside.
He was coming down fast but needed a bit more time.
Carlos felt the teacher grabbing his shoulder and shaking him.
He could not move. He could not react.
There was a drop of saliva escaping from the corner of his mouth.
"My God! What is happening?" she was really frightened now.
"Children, quick, call the principal! Call the nurse!"
Carlos was aware of the panic around him, the teacher screaming, the children running around.
All this was distracting him from concentrating to get back into his body.

A bit too late he realised, that as he had never before succeeded in getting out of his body, Magda had not taught him how to get back.

He was on his own.

The principal arrived, more shouting.

The ambulance arrived.

He was on the stretcher in the ambulance, leaving the school when he arrived back to his body.

"How to get in?"

The body was hollow, empty but completely closed.

No way in.

The oxygen mask on his face and the nurse fussing about did not help the concentration.

"How to get in? There must be a way."

He lay on top of his body with his back feeling the chest, and reaching back grabbed both sides of the body trying to pull himself into it.

It felt the right thing to do, but it did not work.

The body was like a closed bubble and did not let him in.

By this time the ambulance was arriving at the hospital.

Carlos had to hurry. There would be much more distractions in the hospital, making it more difficult to find a way in.

He pulled harder with all his effort concentrated on pulling himself into his body.

There was a sensation of "pop" again and he was in.

The familiar, enclosed feeling was good.

It was relaxing.

Completely exhausted, Carlos fell asleep.

....

"I was going to tell you that it was a very thoughtless thing what you did, but I have changed my mind. It was absolutely stupid. I am very disappointed in you."

"I am sorry Magda. But you have always told me that I should practice wherever I can and that seemed the perfect opportunity."

"I have also taught you to plan things before doing them."

"I am really sorry but it all ended up well. I did find my way back."

"You did not. You did everything upside down. It was an automatic body response that opened the way for you. It was just sheer luck that you got back into your body."

"You mean..."

"Yes. By all rights you should be floating away somewhere unconscious while your body is dying in the hospital"

"Why unconscious? I was feeling fine. More than fine...."

"Carlos! Can you name me a movement or action which does not require any energy?"

"Well, no...."

"Your astral body has no way to produce any energy. It is using your life energy for its actions, which is limited. A permanent separation from the physical body is terminal. You would have died twice as the physical body is not functional without the astral connection."

"I was lucky."

"Very, and hopefully you will remember this for your future adventures."

"I will. You can be sure about it. I have never been so frightened in my life."

"You had reason to be frightened."

"I know. But what about my hospital stay?"

"What about it?"

"How do I explain it?"

"You do not have to. You have been in the hospital for over a week and they have done all the tests they could think of.

Naturally they could not find anything wrong with you."

"They must have made some conclusions."

"Yes. They were talking about heat exhaustion and dehydration, but very vague about it all.
Still, medically you are in the clear."

"What about the school? What about my mother?"

"Well, they all got the medical reports which should satisfy them; still you will carry the stigma on your head that weird "mental" things can happen to you in some conditions. This could be in your favour if someone in the future catches you doing something weird."

"Nice. So from being just weird now I graduated to being a freak."

....

"Carlos, please tell me the truth."

"Mum I always tell you the truth, you know that."

"Yes I know. I know. But this time I really want to know the truth."

"What do you want to know?"

"Stop that Carlos! You know very well what I want to know – what happened? Why did they take you to the hospital?"

"Mum. You got all the medical reports. You know that there is nothing wrong with me."

"I talked to your teacher. She has a different opinion. She says that you were unconscious, unresponsive all the time they took you to the ambulance. That does not sound very healthy to me."

"The doctors said it was a kind of fainting due to the heat. Spectacular to watch, frightening to me but nothing important."

"I find it very difficult to believe that."

"Why not? That was the doctor's opinion. You got the report."

"Carlos. Was it anything to do with what you are practicing during the night?"

"Mum.....you....you have never talked about that."

"I know. I know. Not that I was not aware of it, but after the Calls I have received I was so afraid of the whole situation that I tried to ignore it. That was my way of dealing with it. I was not able to cope with those things. I always knew that it was wrong, but you appeared to be safe and well looked after, so I choose the easier way out."

"So what changed now that you bring it up?"

"That it occurred to me that you are not safe. That changes everything."

"Mum. I am safe. Believe me. I am ok."

"So what really happened there? The truth this time."

"Okay. The truth. It is very simple and very stupid at the same time. I was practicing something I was not supposed to do. Something I did not properly learn how to do and was not supposed to do without supervision. Naturally it went all wrong and my mental and body functions were all disturbed. I had recovered by the time I was in the ambulance."

"That is why the doctors could not find anything wrong with you. Are you completely OK now?"

"Yes Mum. Everything is back to normal. It was all due to my own stupidity and I already had quite a tongue lashing from my tutors."

"They better make sure that you will not do it again!"

"The fright I had made sure of that."

"So they look after you well?"

"Yes Mum. They have been teaching me since before I was born. They are with me constantly.

I can call on them anytime I need them. I really don't know why they are doing it as they do not appear to get anything out of it themselves."

"I would like to meet them. Well, they appear to be a very important part of your life and I am really ashamed that I have ignored for so long that part of your life."

"Mum..... You have changed. A lot."

"You gave me quite a fright and while I was waiting at the hospital for the doctors to tell me if you were still alive, I realised how little I really know about you. It made me question myself, made me question what kind of mother I was."

"You are the best mother I ever had."

"Carlos. This is not a joke."

"What I meant to say was that I would not change you for anyone else. I love you the way you are."

"Thank you Carlos. But I do want to change. I do want to get more involved in your life."

"Mum I am really happy that you want to do that; it's just that I am not sure how to go about it. It is a bit complicated to explain."

"Why don't you let them do the explaining?"

"Okay...they agree to do it. When would you like to meet them?"

"What do you mean they agree to do it? How do you know?"

"Mum, you had better start getting used to the idea that they are able to do things beyond our comprehension."

"I..... I have already had a feeling about that. So when could they come here?"

"Anytime you want them to."

"Carlos, no one can....okay, anytime?"

"Yes."

"What about right now?"

"You are trying to catch me in a lie but it is OK. Right now."

There was knock on the door.

Therezia looked questioningly at Carlos.

"Well, you wanted it right now."

"It is them? But I am not prepared. I am not dressed, there is nothing ready."

"Mum you look fine. Should I open the door?"

"No......I will ....I think."

There was an old woman standing at the door dressed all in black standing very erect with a serious expression on her face.

Just behind her there was a younger man all smiles, dressed simply but very elegantly.

"Hi, I am Magda. This is my friend Steven. Carlos said that you would like to talk to us."

"Well... yes... I am Therezia and please come in."

Therezia was a bundle of nerves, all confused.

Too many unexpected things were happening too fast.

"Please sit down. I...... I really did not expect visitors, I've got nothing prepared."

"We came from quite far away and would be very grateful for a cup of tea."

"Oh, of course. I am a very poor host. I will be back in a minute. Carlos, make sure our guests are comfortable."

Therezia disappeared into the kitchen, very grateful for the breathing time. She needed to pull herself together and present them a composed person as Carlos's mother.

When she came back with the tea on a tray her visitors were sitting at the table with two plates of small cakes in front of them.

"Therezia, Carlos told me that you did not have any time to get ready for visitors so I took the liberty of bringing some cakes with me. I always found that conversation goes easier if

you've got something to munch on."
"They look quite delicious, thank you."
"These are my favourites. I hope you will like them."
They ate in silence for a while
There was an awkward tension in the air until Magda broke
the silence.
"Therezia, let me start the conversation. Although this is the
first time we meet face to face we both know that we have a
long history, going back many years. I do understand that the
present situation is very emotional for you and let me
reassure you that although sometimes it might have appeared
to you differently, we always had you and Carlos's best
interests in mind. We were always your friends from a
distance, and we would like to be your friends face to face
too."
"Thank you. Your presence here kind of proves what you say.
I have many questions for you. I don't know where to start."
"There is no hurry, take your time. The tea is nice and the
chairs are quite comfortable."
"The problem is, that to be able to ask you a question, I have
to know something to ask a question about. I know nothing
about you. I know nothing about your connection with
Carlos. I know nothing about what is happening in my house. I
know that it is mostly my fault, still it is very unsettling that my
son has a life with strangers I know nothing about."
"Believe me; I really understand how you feel. Let me explain
our situation. It could take a bit of time so please be forgiving.
It may appear that I am just rambling on, but I have
to go around a bit in order to get to my point.""Please go ahead. I
really want to know what is happening."
"Okay. Now you probably know or heard about people with
special talents. Someone who can paint wonderful pictures,

someone who can sing, someone who has fantastic memory and is able to memorise full pages of the phone book in minutes. These people can do some things so extremely well that they stand far out from the crowd, from the normal. People are interested in them. They appear on the television, in the newspapers. They are accepted talents, as everyone can paint a little or sing a little.

Hence the person with the exceptional capacity for painting or singing is not so strange.

Now, there are other people, with other, not so well known talents.

People who can perceive your emotions, called empaths, there are people who can move objects at a distance, and this is called telekinesis. Then there are people who can control fire or the wind or other aspects of our environment.

These talents are not as well accepted by everyone.

The more unusual the talent, the less it is accepted by the general populace. People do not like individuals that are different, or who are able to do things they cannot and do not understand.

People fear these individuals and fear is not well tolerated. You must have heard about the burning of witches, the stoning and persecution of monsters and those that were just different?"

"I have heard all about that, but where does Carlos come in to this story?"

"Give me a bit of time please. I will get to that."

"Sorry, please continue."

"People who are different and have unusual talents have limited choices in order to survive.

One of the choices is to hide their talent and live in society as a normal person. This of course is possible only if the difference is not physically visible. The other choice is to hide away, to live in remote areas, where no one can see them.

There is really no other choice.

The person who is different and is known by the people around him, would at first be a subject of interest like a freak, but sooner or later will end up being persecuted and will be unable to survive.

The most affected are the young children that are born different. Aside from facing a life full of difficulties, when they are very young, they do not understand what is happening to them.

Why are they different? Why are people treating them like that? The few that survive childhood with a sane mind will not survive the persecution which will inevitably follow."

"I still do not see....."

"I am getting to that now. Quite a few years ago a group of these special people got together forming a, lets name it a club. The main objective of these people is to find those unusual individuals when they are very young, educate them, teach them about their own capacities, and bring them up as normal, functional members of society. We are part of that "club". Carlos is one of the special children. Carlos was born with fantastic capacities that are far beyond normal comprehension. Leaving him alone, without special supervision, he had no chance to survive his own mental powers. He is such an unusual person that we were aware of his potential birth at the time of the pregnancy with his birth mother. We were expecting him and contacted him before he was born, and, well, the end result you have sitting next to you a normal, functional human being, well-adjusted and living in harmony with society, in spite of his tremendous /capacity."

"Carlos, what do you say to all of this?"

"What do you want me to say Mum?"

"Well, all this is completely new to me and I do not know how to take it."

"Mum, please take it seriously. Everything Magda says is absolutely true and I am the living proof of that."

"What do you mean living proof? Are you.....?"

"Mum, do you want a cake?"

"Carlos, I was....."

One of the small cakes lifted from the table and after a few seconds hesitation started to float towards the astounded Therezia.

"Mum lift your hand please."

The cake slowly descended onto Therezia's extended palm.

"I hope you like that cake."

"You can move things without touching them?"

"Not quite. I do not have that talent. But I can change the weight of things by changing their molecular composition and I can manipulate the temperature and density of the air around them. The end result is the same, just a bit more complicated."

"So you are one of them?"

"Yes Mum, I am one of the freaks,"

"Carlos, if you had two heads and five legs I would not call you a freak. I meant that you are one of the persons Magda was talking about. What you just said did not make any sense to me but your demonstration with the cake really drove Magda's point home."

"Mum, Magda was trying to explain something very complicated in a rather simple way."

"It might be simple for you but it is a rather large mouthful for me to swallow."

"Therezia, do you have any questions?"

"Yes I do Magda, although I am not sure where to start. I do understand what you said about Carlos's position, although I will need a lot of thinking to be able to absorb the meaning of this situation. What I really do not understand is my role in the picture."

"You are his mother; you have to be in the picture."

"I don't mean that. I mean that in the past, much before Carlos was born I got those Calls at night. Was that you?"

"No. Not me personally, but yes, one of our group."

"But why was I contacted? I do not have any special talent."

"You did have very special capacities at birth but you denied them and you have lost them. I am not sure what went wrong but our contact frightened you, causing you a lot of emotional disturbance. We did not have any choice but to break the contact with you."

"So I am completely normal now?"

"Well, I am not sure what do you call normal, but yes you are right. You have the usual talents everyone else has. Still, maybe because you were one of us once, you have the emotional capacity to understand our problems and motives."

"Please give me some time and I will try to understand all I have learned today. Can I have another question?"

"Of course."

"What about you Steven? You did not say a word all the time you were here."

"I am sorry for that Therezia, but you probably noticed that when Magda talks, you do not often have the chance to open your mouth. Okay, okay I did not mean it the way it came out. Besides, what she said was quite clear. I do not have anything to add "

"Thank you Steven, you talked yourself out of that hole quite nicely. Therezia, I would like to get two things out of our meeting today. Firstly, please think upon the things you heard today and ask any questions you want, any time. The second is something personal. I would like you to be my friend and to meet up with you from time to time."

"I would like that very much. One more question?"

"Go ahead."

"Why are you people doing this? I mean looking after Carlos. The way I see it you are putting in a lot of work and I cannot think of any benefit you gain from it."

"It is very simple. We are re-paying a debt. Each of us, when very young, had similar tutors who looked after us. Every time we visit Carlos he is getting deeper in debt himself, a debt that he will have to repay in the future by looking after another child."

"Therezia girl! Are you ready?" -The shouting Pietro rushed in nearly bringing the door in with him.

It took only a few seconds for him to change into a very embarrassed, apologetic person.

"Oh. Hi. I did not know we had visitors."

Therezia was trying to save the moment by making introductions.

"Pietro, these are Magda and Steven, very old friends of mine. Sorry – I meant to say friends for a very long time. Magda this is Pietro, my partner in crime, with very little social skills. Magda and Steven came to visit me after a very long time and I hope their next visit will be a bit sooner."

"Nice to meet you people. I consider my friend anyone who is friendly with Therezia. Sorry for the loud interruption but Therezia seems to have forgotten that we are due to a couple of friends place very shortly."

"The Stevenson's. Sorry dear but I have really forgotten about them. I was so thrilled about my friend's unexpected visit that I did not think about anything else."

"Nice to meet you too Pietro. Do not worry about us as you can see we were half way to the door when you came in. I hope we will have a longer conversation the next time we meet."

....

"What do you think Steven?"

"I do not know Magda. He is very hard to read."

"Yes and that is exactly what I am worried about. He has a formidable mental barrier. I could not get through it. I do not even know if it is a natural barrier or one acquired by special training"

"So what's the problem?"

"Well a natural barrier like this one which appears to be a strong box, is very rare but acceptable. He probably does not even know that he has it. Now, if it is a learned skill, then what is he hiding? That is my problem. With Carlos around we cannot take any chances.

What is your impression?"

"Come on Magda! You could not read him, what do you want me to do?"

"I do not expect you to read him, but you are an empath and I am not. You should be able to pick up some emotions."

"I did not. The moment he walked in I felt an instant dislike towards him, but that was my own reaction. I could not pick up anything from him and I did try."

"Steven, I have learned in the past to take your gut feelings seriously. We'll just have to watch this fellow very closely."

....

It was too hot.

The bed was uncomfortable.

The pillow too high. Or too low.

The blanket scratchy.

Moya was tossing around in her bed without being able to find a comfortable position.

She could not sleep.

It was quiet in the house.

Too quiet.

"Naturally everybody is asleep by now"- the thought appeared to upset her more.

"Of course they are asleep. They can relax. They can be happy, they are not alone."

Father has Therezia. He is so obsessed with her that lately I ceased to exist for him. We used to do all sorts of things together, but not anymore. I sort of disappeared from the landscape.

Although Therezia always tried to be friendly, she was never that close to me, so there is no real loss there.

But Carlos was my friend.

At least I thought he was my friend.

Lately he is also ignoring me.

Like anyone else.

He has no time for anything.

He says he has to study, but why is he studying so much? He is not even very good at school.

What is he studying so much?

He is always in his room.

Alone.

Not even his mother goes in there.

What is he doing there?

He used to be fun. Not anymore.

He probably does not even remember me.

I bet if I would ask him quickly he wouldn't even remember my name."

Moya kicked the blanket off and got out of bed.

She was not sure what she wanted to do but she could not stay in bed anymore.

Tossing and turning.

Being more and more upset about being so lonely in the world, everyone ignoring her.

And Carlos happily asleep.

"Not fair. Why should he be asleep when I can't?"

Moya opened her door very quietly and walked along the long corridor towards Carlos's room.

She stopped outside his room listening.

He was not asleep either.

Moya could hear movements in the room.

Flicking lights under the door.

A strange, stinging smell filtered out.

"Fire!"

Moya burst into the room with a scream coming up her throat but froze after a few steps into the room.

Carlos was sitting at the table with a long copper rod in his hand. The end of the copper rod was on fire.

"Carlos what the hell are you doing?"

"What the hell are you doing in my room?"

"I thought there was a fire in here and wanted to help."

"There is a fire in here but I do not need any help."

"I can see that now. Anyway, what are you doing?"

"Nothing."

"Sure. Nothing. How did you make that metal burn?"

"It is a trick."

"Of course it is a trick. Metal does not burn with a flame like that. What did you put on it?"

"Nothing."

"Sure, then....what made the flame? I saw it."

"The copper."

"Yes, and what was on the copper?"

"Nothing, I told you that. Have a look yourself. The rod is completely clean."

"You wiped it clean."

"I did not."

"I will believe you if you show me the flame again."

"Okay, I will show you, but you have to keep quiet so I can concentrate."

Carlos closed his eyes while holding the metal rod between the two of them.

Visualising the metal particles down to the molecular level.

Increasing the spin of the electrons.

Shifting the protons within the nuclei, increasing the vibration of the particles.

The top of the rod started to heat up.

The excess of energy of the electron spin gave out light.

The tip of the rod was shining brighter and brighter red.

Some of the increasingly vibrating molecules escaped from the main mass and ignited when mixing with the oxygen in the air.

Flame burst out from the top of the rod.

"Okay, I believe you. I do not know how you did that but I believe you. It is a fantastic magic trick."

Carlos opened his eyes.

The fire sizzled out with the rod cooling down fast.

In a very short time the metal rod was cool to touch with practically no marks from the fire.

"A magic trick?"- Carlos took a deep breath to really tell her off.

Then stopped.

It was not a bad idea. And she brought it up herself.

"Yes of course it is. But do not ask how I do it. A magician never reveals his secrets."

"So, this is what you were practicing when you said you were studying. Show me what else you can do."

"I will. I promise, but not now. We had better go to sleep."

It was much easier to sleep now.

Carlos was back in her life.

....

It was hot in the room.

Uncomfortably hot.

The heat woke Carlos up in the middle of the night.

Still half asleep he did not know what was happening but something was not right.

He wanted to turn around to find a more comfortable position.

He tried to turn around.

There was definitely something wrong.

He could not move.

Carlos was fully awake now.

He could not open his eyes.

Could not feel anything wrong with them, they just did not open.

He could not move his fingers or legs.

His chest was moving as he was breathing, but he could not feel the movement.

Carlos decided that he was still asleep and was trying to get into a more comfortable position.

"You are not asleep."

The rasping voice was unmistakable.

Zacharias! What was he doing in his room?

But was he in the room?

"It is really simple Carlos. You are in your room and I am with

you in your room. And no one else is in here. Do not try to call
Magda as you are unable to squeeze your ring. You cannot
move any muscles in your body. You've got good mental
defences, Magda taught you well, however you let your
defences down while you were asleep and it was easy for me
to get full control. That is correct, full control. To demonstrate
this to you I want you to open your mind, completely. NOW!"
Carlos could not resist. His mind was open without any
defences for Zacharias to do whatever he wanted to do.
Or anyone else who wanted to contact him at this moment.
Even Magda. She would be able to see and hear everything
that went on in his room if she wanted to contact him.
But why would she want to contact him at this time?
Maybe even if she would think about him she would pick up
the situation.
"Please, think about me!"
"You don't have to worry about anything. I am not trying to
harm you in any way. I wanted to explain to you our situation,
our group's thinking and this was the only way I could
approach you. I am sure Magda explained to you her way of
thinking about our relationship with the common people, but
you cannot have a free choice unless you know both sides of
the story. You have to agree with that. So please listen and let
me explain things to you. Yes, you have a free choice to join
either side and no, you cannot be independent. You are with
us or against us. I really wish that you choose our side and
no, we cannot allow you to be against us. You are presenting
a potential for so much power that we just cannot afford you
being our enemy.
What will we do? Well, let's go back to that question after you
have listened to what I have to say. Not that you have much
of a choice now.

Okay, let me present you with the facts first, that we, meaning you, Magda, me and the others like us are no monsters or freaks. We are all human beings except we are a new kind.

Just as Homo Sapiens was the next step from our common ancestors, the Primates, our kind is the next step after Homo Sapiens. It is a natural evolution. If you look back on our past evolutionary path, there is a definite progression from the physical towards the mental.

Homo sapiens' supremacy was due to their brain development. Our kind is the next step in the same direction. Now, these are facts, you cannot discuss them. I am just pointing them out to you to clarify our situation.

Simple natural selection, the survival of the fittest. The same thing is happening now. Homo Sapiens is destined to disappear in time. It is inevitable. It is the natural thing to happen.

Except it will not happen soon, not in our lifetime, probably not even for several generations. We are at the very beginning of this process of natural selection.

Everyone knows this. Magda knows this. The only difference that separates us is that Magda's group wants to stand aside and allow the evolutionary process to happen on its own time. Which might take many generations.

In the meanwhile our kind suffers.

Suffers from persecution, is exposed to mental and physical illness. The lucky ones are able to hide their talents and survive in a life of lies. My group does not want to accept this situation for the many generations needed for the natural changes to happen.

Our people want to have a normal life, now.

In the open.

Like everyone else.

And if due to the sapiens nature, this needs violence to happen, we are prepared to use violence. So this is it, in a nutshell. I want you to think about the two approaches and in your own time decide what kind of life you want for yourself and for us in the future. Yes, I can see it in your mind. Magda gave you a lot of detail about what would happen between us and regular people. I can see that you will not change your mind.

Carlos I am really sorry but as I said before we cannot afford you being against us..."

"Hello Zacharias!"

He did not have to turn around to know who was standing behind him.

"Magda! So the little rat managed to call you after all."

"Let him go!"- The soft voice had an incredible amount of threat.

"Magda you know this is nothing personal. You know why I....."

"You knew he is under my care. I take it very much personally."

"Magda please! We were friends once."

"Yes, we were, and because of that you got away with a lot of things. This time you went too far!"

"Magda please...."With a scream of pain, Zacharias fell to the ground clutching
his head.

He stayed there, twitching for a few moments.

Carlos sat up in his bed observing everything with very open eyes, only half understanding what was happening.

After quite a few minutes, Zacharias quietly stood up, dusted his clothes, put on his hat and with a nod of salute left the room.

"You just let him go?"

"Did you want me to kill him?"

"No, of course not but...."

Steven's voice came from the background.

"He is not a threat any more. He will not remember you or anything else that happened here."

"What about later? His friends will just reverse whatever Magda did to him."

"No one can reverse Magda's punishment. Just remember this and make sure you will never upset her."

"Of course I don't want to upset her, she is my friend. But what...?"

"Everything you do has a representation in your brain. Your capacity to speak, to see, to feel, all have a physical seat in your brain. So has your psi capacity. Magda burned out the site for psi capacity in Zacharias' brain. He is a common person now, with no memory or understanding of psi activities. And it is permanent. He will not even recognise his old friends."

Carlos felt relieved with Zacharia's departure however this relief did not last long.

First of all, the memory of what happened kept lingering on. The memory Zacharias being inside his mind, controlling him, making him act like a puppet.

This invading presence made him feel dirty inside and this soiling was hard to remove even with five or six showers a day.

He could not get over this feeling of uncleanliness inside himself.

And this caused him to make a very firm decision. This cannot, will not, happen again. He has to train his defences.

There cannot be another intrusion in his mind.

For the first time, Carlos asked Magda for more work, more training.

And he got it.

He had already learned how to protect his mind from outside forces, but this was nearly impossible to maintain whilst asleep.

How to concentrate on defending himself while asleep?

The answer was more training. More work.

Even Therezia was involved in this training.

Magda gave her a torch or something that looked like a torch. What she had to do was, to point this "torch" at Carlos , anytime day or night, when he was not expecting it.

When his defences were up and strong, nothing happened. If his defences were not strong enough, he received an electric shock.

Not harmful, but quite a nasty one.

Even at night, Therezia would sneak into his room while he was asleep and point the torch at him.

She got really upset about the electric shocks she was giving him but both Carlos and Magda asked her to keep doing it to help his training.

It worked on the same principle as a bed wetting alarm. The bell wakes up the kid in fright every time the bed gets wet, until he learns the control even when he is asleep.

It took Carlos nearly four months of restless sleep and electric shocks to learn to keep his defences up even whilst he was asleep. During this time every waking moment was dedicated to this training.

After the four months both Carlos and Magda slept well, knowing he was safe from any mental invasion.

....

"Come on Carlos!"

"Leave me alone."

"Come on. Do some magic tricks for us."

"I don't do magic tricks."

"Moya says you do."

"Moya's got a big mouth."

"Yes, she does, but she is not lying. She says you have been practicing at home and know some good tricks."

"I have been learning some tricks, but just for myself. I am not doing any shows."

"Come on Carlos. Moya said...."

"Moya should not have said anything and I will have a few words with her as soon as I get home."

"Sorry Carlos, I only wanted to help you."

"How the heck would you help me by telling people I am doing magic tricks?"

"You can do some very neat tricks. I thought you could be more popular if you show them to people."

"How popular?"

"Well, you can't exactly say that you've got friends to spare."

"I do not need friends, especially not the kind who tell on me."

"I said I was sorry. Still I don't understand what the big secret is about doing magic tricks."

"Everything about magic is secret."

"I know that, but what's the problem with people knowing that you are doing magic tricks?"

"I am not ready yet. I need more practice, and every time people ask me to perform and I refuse, does not make me any more popular."

"Okay, okay. I get the point; you don't have to bite me. Just let me know when you are ready. I want to be proud of my magician friend."

....

"I am very proud of you kiddo."

"Thank you Magda, although I am not sure exactly why you are proud of me."

"Every other kid would have taken the opportunity to show off with his magic tricks. You did not."

"Yes, that is all I would need now. To call attention on myself as a kid magician."

"That is exactly what I mean. You did realise how important it is for you to stay in the shadows. Any other kid would have shown off."

"I am not any other kid."

"I agree with you in that and I am quite happy about your being more mature than what you're supposed to be at your age, Just....."

"Just what?"

"Well, although maturity is clearly a survival thing for you, I am not sure it is a good thing all together"

"If you're trying to confuse me you have succeeded. Is maturity a good thing or not?"

"In the situation you happen to be in, you would not survive with a childish behaviour. You are relatively safe now ,as your would-be enemies do not know much about you. So as you have said, calling attention on yourself would not be a healthy thing. But there is another side of the coin too."

"What is the other side?"

"I cannot help the feeling that you are missing out on your childhood. You cannot come back and do it again later. This should not happen to anyone."

"If by childhood you mean running around with the other kids doing silly things, I don't think I am missing much."

"You do not seem to have many friends. Are you comfortable with that?"

"Moya was asking me the same questions today."

"And what about Moya?"

"What do you mean what about Moya?"

"Well who is she to you? Is she a friend, an enemy, or just a person who happens to be around?

"I....I have never really thought about Moya. I remember well that at the beginning I really disliked her, but looking back that was only due to her being a girl. Lately I got quite used to her, probably because she doesn't behave like a girl."

"Got used to her?"

"Okay. She is a friend. As you said I do not have many of them."

"What are your plans about her?"

"Plans? I do not have any plans about her."

"You are living in the same house. How long do you think you can keep your 'magic tricks' a secret form her?"

"I didn't really think about that. I am not sure what to do. I can't just tell her how things are with me."

"You could if she would be sharing the magic with you."

"How is that possible? Could she learn?"

"Not at the extent that you do, but everyone has the capacity to learn providing they have the basic makeup for it. She appears to be a smart girl. The question is, would she be willing to put in the work and the energy?"

"I think she would. She is fascinated by ESP ad UFOs and all that stuff."

....

"Carlos, I am not sure what you are talking about."

"All that magic stuff you are talking about. The things the

witches and the wizards do at the movies."

"Yes, I like all that stuff. What about it?"

"Well, would like to be able to do stuff like that?"

"I would love to. I used to daydream about that kind of stuff. I still do sometimes, but that stuff is just in the movies. Not real."

"What if it was real?"

"It would be fantastic, providing I could do it."

"Would you like that?"

"Carlos. What the heck are you talking about? You sound serious but you're talking about nonsense."

"Come on. Just go along with me. Pretend that all those magical things are real. Would you like to be able to do magic?"

"Of course I would. I would do anything to be magical.""Even if you would have to learn it, with an awful lot of hard

work, just like in school."

"You mean a school for witches?"

"Not quite, but that is the idea. Suppose it would be possible to learn real magic, not just tricks. But it would take a lot of work and effort to do it. Would you?"

"Would I what?"

"Would you be able to put in the effort and work to learn?"

"I said I would. If it was real it would be the most important thing in my life. But it is not real, so just tell me what the point of this conversation is?"

Carlos did not answer.

He just put an ice block on the palm of his hand.

In a few seconds there was only a puddle of water in his palm.

"Big deal. You melted the ice. I could do that. Maybe not that fast, but I could do that."

The water appeared to be moving, then solidified. In a few

seconds there was a cube of ice once again in the palm of his hand.

"I definitely could not do that. It's a very neat trick."

Moya was scratching her right knee while she was watching the ice cube.

Then the left one.

Then the right one again.

Then the left one.

"Carlos, are you doing this?"

"Am I doing what?"

"This itchy business."

"Is it a trick?"

"I am not sure what you are doing."

"I am trying to show you the things I have learned to do with my mind and convince you that you can learn them too."

"Are you trying to tell me that all that magic stuff in the comic books is real?"

"Well not all of it but part of it, yes."

"And I can learn to do all that stuff?"

"A small part of it at least."

"That is good enough for me. I am still not sure that you are not pulling my leg but I am willing to try. When do we start?"

"Now hold on! Not so fast. There are a lot of things to consider first."

"Such as? You know if I want something I am willing to work for it."

"I know that. But what about secrecy? Will you be able to keep this a secret from every one? Even your father?"

"Not a word?"

"Not a word."

"What is the point of this secrecy? My father would be happy if I learned something new."

"That is not the point. You will be able to do things other people cannot. No one will understand. You would be a freak and eventually an outcast."

"My father wouldn't think I was a freak."

"Your father probably not, but if he knew, other people would too."

"So, are you a freak?"

"I would be if anyone would know."

"What if I tell about you now?"

"You would be the freak as nobody would believe you."

"I think I can see your point. Okay I promise, I swear and anything else you want. Let's suppose all this that you are saying is true, what's next?

"The next thing is to meet your teacher. Say hi to Magda."

....

"It has to be okay. It just has to be."

Carlos had problems accepting the changes in his life provided by this new development with Moya.

Walking home from school he was concentrating trying to work out the future complications these changes brought.

In principle, at first it appeared a good idea.

To have someone of his own age to talk to, to share his thoughts with. To be able to open his mind freely and not have to be careful with every word he said, not to be afraid of unwillingly revealing something he should not.

And Moya was a good choice to be this person.

Actually, Moya was the only choice. Carlos could not think of anyone else who could be this person.

His mother was involved now also, which was good in a way, but Carlos did not reveal everything to her.

Partly because being his mother, some situations could be

embarrassing, partly because he was not quite sure if she could be trusted with some of the information.

She wasn't the kind of person to keep secrets.

Especially not from Pietro, who was another unknown in the equation.

He had done nothing wrong , but Magda still could not establish if he was trustworthy.

Moya was different. Carlos trusted her.

He knew that when she wanted something she would get it even if she had to go through hell to do so.

And even though she had a big mouth, she was able to keep it shut when she needed to.

The whole thing appeared to be good except that it added an extra work load to his already hectic schedule.

Besides his own training, the school work, the keeping up of appearances in the neighbourhood by being a "normal kid", now he would have to assist in Moya's training.

He was not sure what this would involve, but expected to have a role in it.

So far he had nothing to do. Except the nightly "Calls" Moya started to receive, nothing else had changed.

He was interrupted in his concentration by loud horns and someone grabbing his shoulder and pulling him back forcibly. "Where do you think you're going?"

For a moment Carlos did not know what was happening. He was only aware that he could not move, being restricted by the strong arms holding him.

He came to his senses very fast when he looked up at the old, winkled face of the man holding him.

Zacharias!

How could he...?

Carlos was so confident in his mental defences that he

sometimes forgot about his physical environment.

That is why the old man was able to approach him without the alarm bells going off.

But still, Zacharias had a special mental signature which should have triggered his defences.

The man was smiling at him, but Carlos already learned not to trust a face with a smile.

Especially not Zacharias.

He was about to squeeze his ring to call Magda when something stopped him.

Zacharia's eyes. They were smiling.

Carlos had also learned that the eyes usually told the truth.

A person could lie, pretend with his face, voice, attitude but the eyes could not be controlled.

And Zacharia's eyes had a friendly smile.

"It is highly recommended to look around before you try to cross the road."

"What do you mean?"

"Looks like you are still half asleep. Didn't you hear all that honking? You nearly gave a heart attack to that poor truck driver by stepping off the kerb right in front of his truck." With a friendly tap on his shoulder the old man pushed him away.

"Go on your way, but keep your eyes open."

With a deep sigh of relief Carlos started to run towards home.

It was Zacharias.

But it was a different Zacharias. He did not remember anything about his past or anything about him.

....

Meanwhile, Moya was not a very happy girl.

She woke up with the feeling that something important had

happened during the night and that she missed it all.

This was not really new for her as lately she woke up with similar feelings quite often.

She also felt unclean, soiled inside and exposed.

It was a feeling very difficult to define but she definitely did not like it.

At the same time she also felt disappointed.

After all that talk about her training she expected something like she had seen at the movies. That magical kids were going to the school of wizards to learn spells and incantations, to use magic wands, to change drinking cups into rats.

Nothing like that has happened.

Actually no training, nothing has changed.

Okay, both Carlos and Magda told her that she was not ready for proper training yet, that her brain had to mature and that this would happen whilst she was asleep. As far as she was concerned – this was still nothing.

Carlos felt sorry for her and wanted to help but Magda stopped him.

"She is not ready yet, don't push her."

"She does not know what is happening."

"You know what is happening. She was born with quite a good psi capacity, but as it was not used, her brain settled in a non psi mode. I have to manipulate, actually produce physical changes in her brain to get it ready for her training."

"I did not know that you can actually produce physical changes."

"Did you not? You actually changed your mother's brain connections before you were born."

"I have never done anything to my mother."

"I do not mean Therezia. I mean Sarah."

"Oh that. I really did not know what I was doing. Parts of those connections just did not feel right, so I changed them."

"Yes, you did that and very drastically changed her life."

"I had often wondered about that. I have this feeling that her early dying had something to do with those changes."

"Why do you say that?"

"Well, with today's medicine no one should die in childbirth. Besides the way she was saying goodbye to Therezia would imply that she was expecting it to happen."

"She did not just expect it to happen. She wanted it to happen."

"Why would she want to die?"

"She did not actually want to die; she just did not want to live the life which was ahead of her."

"You are trying to confuse me again."

"Carlos, Sarah was born with tremendous psi capacities; however, these could not surface as her unfortunate genetic make-up provided her with a body and a brain unable to function properly. By fixing up the faults in her neural connections you did not just give her normal thinking and communication capabilities, but also opened the way to fantastic psi activities.

She knew exactly what was happening and what her life ahead would be. Her departing was by choice."

"Well, obviously I do not have her fantastic psi capabilities as I've got no idea what you are talking about."

"She was born with a genetic malformation which gave her an inferior body and impaired mind. The mark of Down's syndrome was obviously visible on her face for everyone to see.

All her doctors knew about her condition. Then her mental state suddenly changed, surprising all the doctors with her surging intellect.

This was so unexpected and unexplained that the medical people could not have left this un-investigated. She would be investigated by doctors, medical teams, hospitals and any scientific institute available. Sooner or later they would have discovered her psi capacities, then she would be a freak and a guinea pig for the rest of her life."

"Why could she not hide the new her?"

"Because she was already out in the open. She was well known first as a mentally impaired person, then she got to be known by her unexplained change. She was out in the open with no way back."

"So it was my fault that she died?"

"It was also your fault that she had a few months of life worth living."

"Not really a fair exchange."

"It was for her. She could have easily unmade the change you have done and be back to her previous life. She refused to do that."

"I still feel guilty."

"Don't be. I am sure she was very grateful for the changes you made."

....

Therezia had problems of her own.

She was torn by two separate worlds and she did not know which way to go.

She could not bring those two worlds together. In one hand, she was quite happy about finally understanding Carlos and being part of his life. She was impressed by his achievements and very proud of her son.

The problem was all this secrecy stuff.

Therezia could not fully understand the need for this secrecy but knew that Carlos and Magda took it very seriously.

She had to follow suit.
On the other hand, there was Pietro.
Therezia really liked Pietro and he appeared to return her feelings.
She expected to have a long term relationship with him, to form a family with Moya and Carlos.
A happy family where, people loved and trusted one another.
How can she then keep a secret from Pietro?
She even talked to Magda about this problem.
They were meeting quite frequently now.
The two women, although they were completely different in every possible way, appeared to like each other's company.
Therezia admired the old woman because of her vast knowledge of just about everything and the serious, dedicated way she carried out her fairly complicated life.
Magda liked Therezia's uncomplicated way of seeing the world, and was amazed by her productions in the kitchen.
Therezia opened a new world for her, things she had never experienced before.
The things so natural and ordinary for Therezia, like shopping, talking to the neighbours, having a snack in a café, or just plain strolling in the park, were all unfamiliar to Magda.
She had a long life behind her but all of it dedicated to work or study,-she never had time for life's simple, daily pleasures.
Therezia was teaching her to enjoy the moment.
She took Therezia's problem seriously.
"Look Therezia, I cannot see any choice for you. We are talking about Carlos's life here. You know that some very powerful people are looking for him and you know the reasons why. I explained all this to you. Carlos is too young to protect himself and we cannot be there every minute of every day to save him. His only protection, the only way he can survive is

to hide, to not to be discovered

Pietro is a nice man, he seems to be okay but we really do not know him that well. I would trust him with the key to my house but not with Carlos's life.

You can see my point, can't you?"

"Yes, I can see your point about people not knowing about Carlos, but Pietro is not just people. He is part of this family."

"Yes, but a very new part. A practically unknown part."

"You trusted me and Moya with this knowledge."

"Yes, but that is different. You are his mother. You love him. Who could I trust with Carlos if not you? And you are needed to help Carlos grow up."

"And Moya?"

"Moya is different again. Being a young child her mind is open to me. I know her likes and dislikes in every detail. I know exactly what she would do and what she is able to do. Based on that, I know I can trust her.

Also her presence is important. We have to be very careful about Carlos's mental development, a lot of things can go wrong during his growing up. With such a power in his hands his emotional and mental state is crucial.

Lately he's had some problems with his concentration; I put that down to being alone. To not having anyone of his age to talk to, to freely discuss his problems with.

He needed someone to share his secrets and Moya is the perfect person to be his companion."

"You seem to be planning everything in detail. Don't you do anything by emotion, without logical thinking?"

"Therezia, I cannot afford emotions, not when we talk about Carlos.

He is the work of my life. I dedicated myself, together with Steven and a few other people in order to bring him up as a powerful, emotionally balanced person."

"Carlos appears to be a very important person."

"Potentially, yes. Carlos, grown up with the right balance of power and frame of mind could be a very, very important person.

You will know what I mean in a few years."

....

Carlos was not happy this day

There was something wrong.

Since he woke up this morning, he had this consistent apprehension that something bad was about to happen.

He did not know what, but it was about to happen.

Carlos never had this feeling. Nothing quite this strong.

The feeling really disturbed him. Calling Magda for advice did not help. It just made him worry more.

"To perceive future events is not your don. However, after all the training you have undertaken to open your mind, it is possible that you are picking up wisps of something important that is going to happen. I do take this very seriously as a warning but there is nothing you can do about it.

Just wait, observe, and be prepared.

Sometimes, probably very soon, you should be able to get more information about the nature of this future thing.

Please let me know the moment you know anything else."

So, just wait and see.

Magda's confirmation about the possible reality of his feelings just made things worse. She turned a vague feeling into reality, into something to fear.

"Thank you Magda!"

So he waited, feared, and waited again.

And nothing happened.

Carlos went to school, went home, -still nothing happened.

He was sitting at the table eating the sandwich his mother prepared for him while trying to avoid her questions about what was wrong with him.

She was also worried about Moya who was late coming home.

Luckily her back was turned towards him when Carlos was hit by this mental scream.

A scream of panic, a scream for help.

Then nothing.

Nothing more except this overpowering fear which now had a cause.

Moya.

Magda was at his side before he could finish squeezing his ring.

"I wish I could do this teleporting thing you do, Magda."

"You will be able to, eventually, after a few more years of training. Now, what did you get?"

"This scream from Moya, nothing else."

"Present it to me just the way you got it."

Carlos concentrated, recalling the scream, every aspect of it. The sound, the emotion, the panic it carried, the impact it caused on him-then passed the whole mental package to Magda.

"Give it to me again."

Magda concentrated, analysing the scream message.

"Yes, it is Moya. She is panicking but not in physical danger for the moment. There also appears to be some visual images. Give it to me again Carlos."

"Yes, a black van, she is inside, at the back. Two men in the front, one young and one older.

Their minds are disgusting. I know where they are.

Carlos,-hold my hand."—They were on a deserted country road.

The sun was setting but there was enough light to see the fast approaching van.

"Carlos, blow the left front tyre."

It was a simple thing to do.

Carlos concentrated on the rubber molecules, making them vibrate faster and faster.

The heat produced melted part of the tyre.

The van, momentarily losing control, stopped on the side of the road.

Two men got out, looking perplexed at the melted tyre.

'Carlos, get rid of them."

"Me? How..?"

"I leave it to you but be rather quick."

Carlos concentrated.Water drops appeared in the air around the two men.

More and more water.

It was like a very heavy rain, just around them.

Both men appeared to be chocking, grabbing their throats, gasping for air.

In a few moments both men were unconscious, lying on the ground.

"It is enough Carlos, do not kill them. By the way, it was a good choice."

Moya was tied up in the back of the van.

Tense, her eyes wide open but she reacted quite calmly when she saw them.

"Thank you for coming for me, I kind of expected it. These two creeps had very nasty intentions. By the way, what happened to them?"

"They just decided to go to sleep."

"I saw them through the window. They were chocking."

"So would you if there was no oxygen in the air around you."

"All I saw was some heavy rain. How..?"

"Carlos here used up the oxygen around them by forming water. The more oxygen poured in from around, the more rain fell. If there is no oxygen in the air around you, you lose consciousness rather quickly. We are kind of used to breathing."

"They are moving. They are starting to wake up."

'Yes they do. It is time for us to go. We can use their van to get home. It is more comfortable."

"And just leave them here?"

"Why not?'

"They are criminals. They wanted to do nasty things to Moya. They should not just get away with it."

"They did not. Moya is safe now."

"And them? Should they not...?"

"Be punished you mean? What do you suggest, calling the police?"

"Well, not that. There are a few things here we could not quite explain. But just letting them go..."

"They will not get away Scott free. I kind of cooked their genitals. They will not be a danger to any girl in the future."

....

So all this frightening episode had a happy ending,

Everyone was satisfied with the end result.

Well, nearly everyone.

Petro and Therezia of course were told what had happened, although not in every detail.

And they were happy to get Moya back safe.

Magda, although not happy about not foreseeing and preventing the situation from happening, was satisfied with the end result.

For Carlos this was a learning experience and was quite

satisfied with the way everything happened, especially after Magda complimented him for the way he handled things.

So everyone was happy.

Everyone except Moya.

For her it had been an intensely frightening experience and was very hard for her to get over it.

For a few days she did not leave the house, stayed always in her room, afraid to go out.

She was afraid of the darkness, noises and sudden movements.

The others understood the situation and left her alone to work out the emotional issues.

Moya knew that everyone else was there to offer help but was grateful for the breathing space.

Aside from being afraid and feeling deeply disturbed by what happened, Moya was angry.

Very angry.

Angry with herself for not being able to control the situation, angry with the two men who kidnapped her with foul intentions and angry with the system, the people on the street who allowed those two men to grab her and push her into the van in plain daylight.

But mainly she was angry with her own weakness and decided that this just cannot, would not, happen again.

She demanded that Magda teach her how to defend herself.

She wanted a weapon; something powerful to swat her next would be attackers.

Magda , though in agreement with the need, was not going to give a powerful weapon to a twelve year old.

"You will have plenty of opportunities to destroy anything you want later in your training, when I am able to trust that you have the maturity to decide what to do."

Eventually they came to a compromise.

During the next few weeks, Moya learned new mental tricks. She became able to emit emotions which made her so disgusting, so repulsive to everyone around her, that people had to flee, unable to tolerate her proximity.

Moya learned the mental trick very fast and the acquired feeling of security, the knowledge that no one could overpower her again, brought back the old Moya, the happy-go lucky twelve year old who could once again enjoy Carlos's company.

....

"No Mum, it has nothing to do with me.

They were just two creeps who wanted to have some fun with a young girl.

No Mum, they did not pick Moya because she is close to me.

Moya just happened to be there when those characters were prowling around. It could have happened to any other girl, it is just that it was Moya who was there.

No, it will not happen again.

Moya has her own protection now and also has a ring to call Magda if she needs her.

No Mum, you do not have to worry about me. I can protect myself.

Okay, okay, I know that there are people looking for me but this episode with Moya had nothing to do with that.

They were not part of the people who are after me.No Mum, I do not know who is after me, that is why I have to

be always alert.Yes Mum, I know that it did happen before, but then I was not

aware of what was happening and was not careful.

Yes Mum, I am very careful now.

Yes Mum, I am practicing and learning every day.

I am also helping Moya.

No Mum, I do not think that you are a bad mother.

I think you are a wonderful mother. You are always doing the best you can.

No, I do not think that your best is not enough.

I know. I know that you cannot help me in these things but you are not supposed to.

That is not your role. Your role is to be our mother, the best mother you can possibly be and you are doing a fantastic job at that.

No Mum, Magda is not my mother, Magda is my teacher.

Of course she knows more than you do, she knows more than everyone here all together.

She is teaching me, that is her role.

You are my Mother that is your role.

Yes Mother, that is the way I feel and please do not change. I like my Mother the way she is now."

....

"Magda, this is very frustrating. Why is that I can't talk to her properly?"

"What do you mean properly?"

"You know. The mental talk. The way I talk to you."

"Moya is not ready for that. You have to be patient with her."

"What do you mean not ready? She is at the same age as I am."

"That is true, except for the fact that she has had four months training and you have had thirteen years."

"Thirteen years? I am just over twelve."

"True again, except that you have forgotten that we have been talking since well before you were born."

"You are right, again, I had forgotten about that. So, will she be able to talk to us?"

'She will. She is a smart girl with a good mind. Just give her time."

"What about my mother? She had no training at all."

"Can she mind speak?"

"Sort of. Quite a few times it happened that I talked to her mentally by accident, and she heard me."

"Did she understand what she was hearing?"

"Not really. She always assumed that I was vocalizing and responded with sound speech.

Also, sometimes when she was very upset, she sent out thoughts that I could pick up."

"Obviously she has some latent psi capacities. I think we should just leave her alone, without disturbing things."

"And what about Moya?"

"What about her?"

"I mean, what should I do with her? Should I show her things, or teach her things?"

"Definitely not. There is nothing you can do there. Moya is not at the stage where she can learn things. At this stage all what we are doing is stimulating the development of her capacities. When she has her eyes open, then she can learn how to read."

CHAPTER FOUR

"Your Excellency, I have some strange news for you."

"I am listening."

"This morning I bumped into Zacharias, accidentally, on the street."

"What did he have to say? He has not reported for some time now."

"Nothing, Your Excellency."

"What do you mean nothing? He was given a very specific task to perform. How is he going with that?"

"I do not know, Your Excellency. He did not say."

"So what did he say?"

"Nothing, Your Excellency. He did not even recognize me."

"Harold, you had better start explaining yourself."

"I can't explain it. He was like a different person. He did not recognize me at all. When I tried to read him, I could not even connect."

"Come on, man, what do you mean you could not connect? What is wrong with you?"

"There is nothing wrong with me. There was nothing to connect to. He had no psi capacity at all."

"Are you sure that he was the right person?"

"Yes. He was Zacharias all right. All the character signs were there proving his identity, still, no psi activity at all."

"Was he suppressed? Was there any positional mental block in his mind? You could have undone those."

"Yes, I could have, but there was nothing like that there. The psi site in his brain was missing as though it was never there. He was a completely common person." "Well, he was not like that before and you know it. It is fairly simple to put a block to someone's psi capacity, but to actually remove the physical site of it in the brain,-very few are able to do that."

"Magda could do that."

"Yes, curse her, she could do that. And if she did, and if it was her who wiped Zacharias clean, it would mean that he managed to find the boy."

"We have been trying to do that for a long time."

"I know. And he has to be close. If the wiped out Zacharias was turned loose in this area, the boy has to be right under our nose."

"We failed to find him so far."

'Well, if Magda is looking after him you will not find him. Did you try following her to the boy?"

'Of course, Your Excellency, but as you said, she is too good. Her tracks are clean, impossible to follow. She should be on our side."

'I wish, but she was one of the Originals who organized the separation of our people into two factions based on our opinion of the untalented persons."

"One of the Originals? It cannot be. How old is she?"

"I do not know, but she was not very young at that time either."

"But that was..."

"Yes, a very long time ago. but if someone were able to remove physically the psi component of Zacharias's brain, then that someone would also be able to fix imperfections in her own body."

"That would mean...."

"Yes, a very long life. The important thing is that a very long life implies a lot of knowledge, a lot of experience."

"What she obviously has."

"Yes, damn her, and she got to look after that boy."

"I am still not clear about why that boy is so important."

"You know about the prophecy."

"Yes, your Excellency. I know about the prophecy. The powerful leader who by force will unify our factions and lead humanity into the future. Yes. I know the story."

"You are missing he main point. That future involves a friendly coexistence of talented and not talented people."

"It is just a prophecy. Certainly at this age you would not..."

"I would not believe in a prophecy? Magda and her group is working hard to make it a reality."

"That makes the whole thing more serious. Still, I can't understand how they can choose a life of hiding amongst the common people, denying the rights nature have given them."

"This is where we come in. We do not want to wait several generations until the natural selection gives us our rights. We want it now. We want to live our lives in the open,without fear of persecution. If there is no other way, we are prepared to use violence."

"It would mean very large casualties."

"Probably, but just to the common people. Natural selection would eliminate them anyway in time, we would just hasten the process."

"And where is the boy coming into the picture? Do not tell me that you believe in the prophecy."

"You should be taking it seriously too. Not as a prediction of the future but as a prediction of a possible future. Something which might happen and we do not want it to happen. You can not just ignore it, especially when you know that important people are working to make it happen."

"But why this particular boy?"

"Well, if we take the prophecy seriously as a possible future, then we have to take seriously its details also."

"'What details?"

"In the prophecy, as you know, there is a very detailed description of the time, the place and the circumstances of the birth of this leader person. We are looking for the boy that fits this description."

"Does this person exist?"

"Yes, he is around. Somewhere close, somewhere under our nose. We've just failed to find him so far."

....

Senior Silvio Horace Robert Gutierrez was not happy with the world around him.

He did not like his routine being disturbed and his present situation really changed his plans for the day.

His rather voluminous body felt uncomfortable sitting on the hard wooden chair and staring at the thin female form across the desk did not help the situation.

A stupis female, at that.

Not that the present situation was strange to him.

He had been summoned to the principal's office quite a few times before, and always for the same reason.

Oscar, his son, was causing problems again.

The same problem again and again, and he did not know how to handle the situation.

Oscar was a good boy.

He always behaved well and as far as his father was concerned he was doing nothing wrong.

The stupis were the real problem.

It was their fault that Oscar had to hide his natural, God given talent and if someone got burnt it was their fault for not getting out of the way.

What else could a pyrokinetic boy do?

They were supposed to burn things. They were supposed to

make fires and practice their control of the talent.

How else could they grow up with good pyrokinetic control?

Oscar was not twelve years old yet, and his father was proud of his achievements.

Only last week his son showed him how he could send the fire along the living room without burning the carpet.

It was quite an achievement for a twelve year old.

Naturally at school he was not able to show his talent, he had to hide his capacities.

The stupis could not know what he was able to do.

Stupis was their secret name for people with no special talents, people who did not understand what psi capacities were.

The name meant someone inferior, someone who really had no excuse to exist, but being the large majority at the moment, they had the balance of power, they made the laws, and these laws, mainly unwritten, said that if you were different in any way, you were treated as freaks, your life was made miserable. By them.

The stupis.

So it did not matter how superior to them you felt in the inside, the simple fact of this majority, implied that you had to hide your superiority and hide your talent.

You had to pretend that you were one of them.

One of the stupis.It was a very degrading feeling and the only thing which made

it supportable was the knowledge that this would change. Not tomorrow, not next year, but eventually.

The number of people with psi capacities was getting larger.

Slowly but constantly and inexorably.

And when there are enough of them....

But none of that helped him in the present situation.

To break his daily routine, sitting there in front of that stupis female and listening to her badmouthing his son, well, it was very difficult to swallow.

To make things worse, he had to smile, had to be friendly to her while all his insides yearned to burn her to cinders.

Just because a girl at school got a little bit burned.

A stupis girl. Who cared?

Oscar was making a small fire in the classroom while nobody else was there. No one would have known about it had that girl not walked in unexpected.

So she got burned. So what?

A stupis girl at that.

It was not really a big burn but the school made a big thing about it.

Again.

This time the principal insisted that Oscar see a psychiatrist.

And he had no alternative but to accept.

Otherwise they would expel him from the school and it would be difficult to go anywhere else with the label of "psychologically disturbed" printed on his son's forehead.

His son labelled as psychologically disturbed.

By a stupis.

This school really deserved to be burned down.

The stupis across the desk did not realise how close to it she was.

At least they gave him the choice of psychiatrist.

He had to find one with an understanding of psi capacities.

There must be one around.

The psi community was slowly infiltrating every level of this stupis society.

One day...hopefully not too far away...

....

And Oscar was a good boy. He really was.
He obeyed all the rules. He tried to blend in.
He really tried.
He was tall and strong. He enjoyed all physical activities, all
kind of sports, and was good at them.
He was sought after by all the teams as his performance was
respected.
By all the rules he should have had a lot of friends.
That was not the case, however.
Aside from the sporting activities, no one sought his company.
Oscar had no close friends, no one to talk to, and no one to
share his problems with.
He felt very lonely. All the time.
He could not get close to his classmates, how could he?
They were all just stupis.
They were really not worth to have as friends.
Oscar felt uncomfortable in their company. He tried not to
show it but people around him could not help but pick up his
feelings of superiority, to feel themselves inferior in his eyes.
He could not help it.
After all, they were all just stupis.
Unable even to imagine psi life, the superior feeling arriving
from controlling the elements.
To have fire dancing in the palm of his hands.
To control the slow or fast burning of objects.
To feel the power of...but the stupis could not understand any
of this.They were just stupis. And he, the pyrokinetic, had to hide
all
this power, all this capacity.
He had to pretend to be one of them.
A stupis.
It was so degrading.

Very difficult to tolerate.

Sometimes, when all this low feeling got too heavy, Oscar made a little fire, just for himself.

Hidden, so no one could see it. Just to feel normal again.

Just to prove to himself that in reality he was not one of them. Not a stupis.

Most of the time it made him feel better.

Sometimes it misfired, just like the last time when that girl unexpectedly walked in on him.

He got distracted, losing control of the fire.

So she got burned. Just a little bit, really.

The school made a big thing out of it.

The whole thing was so unfair.

As though it was his fault.

Like it was something important.

After all it was just a stupis. So what if she got a little burned.

And on top of it, it was her fault. She caused him to lose control.

He had done nothing wrong. He was supposed to practice with fire. That is what pyrokinetics do.

True, no one knew that he was pyrokinetic, but that was also their fault.

It was their rules, their laws that made him hide his talent.

They made the rules. Just because they were the majority.

How unfair.

Father always said that this would change. He did not say when but he was sure it would be soon.

It was only fair that it should happen.

Oscar knew that there were people working on the problem, on making the psi supremacy a reality, on not having to wait until the natural selection eliminated the stupis, as had always been the case with an inferior race.

It will happen.

But for now, they had to hide, had to pretend that they were "normal", to pretend they also were stupis.

Just because of their numerical majority.

Oscar considered himself lucky that his father did not side with the school. He did receive a telling off, but only for not being careful enough, for getting caught.

He knew that his father understood, as he himself went through the same kind of problems and that, when he was the same age, he was caught more often than Oscar had been.

Luckily he was only punished as a misbehaving boy and his true nature had never been discovered.

Many times this was just out of pure luck and Oscar learned from his father's mistakes.

He was more careful.

His father also tried to help by getting him friends of his own kind.Robert was a little bit older than Oscar and lived only about three streets away, although he went to a different school.

Robert was telekinetic, he could move objects without physically touching them.

He was not very good at it; he had problems with his control. Maybe due to not practicing enough, but he kept pushing things away, knocking them over without wanting to do so, or dropping things when he was trying to levitate them.

Naturally, this got him into a lot of trouble at school as it was hard to explain things constantly dropping to the floor around him.

He was classified as a really bad boy at school.

There was also Angelina who lived nearly at the other side of the city. She was an empath, she could feel the emotions of people around her.

Even if they were stupis.

She was quite efficient when she wanted to read someone, was able to pick up very deep, intimate feelings, however her control failed in blocking out unwanted emotions.

Quite often, even if she did not want it to happen, she felt the turbulent emotions around her. She would feel suddenly intensely happy, angry or sad without any apparent reason.

It was very hard for her to hide these intense emotions she felt from people all around her, especially at school.

Everyone thought that she was a "little strange."

At least she was not classified as being a naughty girl. The three of them sometimes got together and had a very

good time.

At least in each other's company, they did not have to pretend, they could behave normally, be their real selves.

It did not happen very often as all three went to a different school, but as their parents met more or less regularly, they at least had this occasional relief from the daily routine of having to hide their true selves.

Hiding from stupis.

Have to pretend that they were like them.

Stupis.

....

Angelina had a bad night. She could not get to sleep.

The neighbours were fighting again, and although the screaming and shouting was screened out by the closed windows, the waves of anger and hatred penetrated through the brick wall.

How could two people hate each other so much and still stay together.

Angelina was not able to screen out those invading emotions.

Her receptive mind was absorbing all the mental waves

around her and she felt their anger and hatred as though being her own.

She had been training a long time now to learn to screen out the unwanted emotions but her control still failed her sometimes.

Especially when she was asleep.

Agnes, her tutor, was guiding her nightly training in using and controlling her talent but the young mind was still unable to cope with the onslaught of mental energies.

Agnes put a lot of time and effort in her training but sometimes, on nights like this, she had to be physically present to protect Angelina with her own mental barrier.

She really hoped that her pupil's control would be strong enough soon so that they both could have some rest.

She was a good girl, really, working, practicing very hard, and was constantly improving.

Only on nights like this with particularly strong influences, she needed help.

Agnes remembered the suffering Angelina went through .

It started practically before she was born.

The extraordinary potency of the receptive mind absorbed all emotions from around her, enjoying the feelings of love and affection, but there was far more anger and hatred in the world and distance appeared not to be a barrier.

Her parents, both empaths, helped with their own mental barriers, but they were no match for the intensity of their daughter's receptive capacity.

Agnes practically had to live with them to be able to help at all.

The invading waves of emotions also affected the baby's physical development. Angelina was born early and with a very low birth weight. The first few years of her development

were marked with recurrent illnesses, headaches and
nightmares.

Although her mental training started before she was born, she
was about eight years old before she was able to control her
receptive capacity enough to not to affect her physical
health.

She started to put on some weight, colour on her cheeks and
was starting to participate in the physical activities of children
of her age.

Now, approaching her twelfth birthday, she was fine, coping
well at school although avoiding close proximity with her
classmates, who classified her as moody and strange but
still accepted her as she was.

She needed help from Agnes less and less frequently.

....

It was a good day for Robert.

It was his eleventh birthday and it already started well.

His mother let him sleep until late which was very unusual.

Robert only woke up when the sunlight from the window hit
his face.

It was a nice feeling, a luxurious feeling just lying in bed,
stretched out under the warm blanket, not having to hurry to
do something.

On the days when he did not have to get up for school his
mother always had some chores for him to do so he could not
stay in bed.

So he was not used to this fantastically nice, lazy feeling in
bed.

Robert enjoyed the feeling of extra calmness but after a while
started to feel guilty. Specially after noticing the faint noises of
activity in the house.

By the time he got to the kitchen his breakfast was on the

table, only his, as everyone else had already finished and were going about their daily routines.

Robert was looking forward to the rest of the day as his father always made a big deal about birthdays.

Still feeling a bit sluggish, he made his cup and plate float to the kitchen sink.

At home he did not have to worry about people seeing him doing things. Everyone in his family were doing it and were very careful not to be noticed by outside people.

Not by the stupies.

But they never came to this house.

His father being the Chief of Police, they had quite a busy social life but stupies were never in the house.

They were not invited here. Father always said that each should stick to his own kind, and stupies were definitely not their kind.

Outside the house everyone was nice to them, pretending to be one of them.

One of the stupis.

You could be very nice to a puppy or a horse without feeling that you were of the same kind.

Luckily they were not like Angelina, they could not pick up how they really felt about them.

Robert always felt that Angelina's talent was very useful although hard to control. Being always clear about people's feelings towards you could be very helpful in deciding who really was your friend.

Not like his talent, the telekinesis.

Okay, it was fun sometimes to move objects with your mind, to not having to bend down when you dropped something, or not having to reach up to get something no matter how high or how heavy they were.

But he could not use his talent anywhere outside the house. A few times he was nearly caught at school. Like the time when he moved the chair as his teacher was just about to sitdown. The result was spectacular but also he was very close to being exposed.

He had to hide his talent. He had to blend in, to pretend to be one of them.

A stupis.

It was a very degrading feeling but his father hammered the importance of hiding into his head again and again.

He also promised that it would not be like this forever.

Their people were slowly occupying all the important positions, like him being the Chief of Police, and when the power will be in their hands, they would make the change.

Robert was not sure about the nature of this change but was really looking forward to openly using his talent.

It would be real fun.

But not yet. His father made sure that he accepted this idea as his own.

It took him a while.

Like when he was about seven years old and his father caught him playing with this beautiful metal robot.

It made clicking sounds when moving; his glass eyes flashed with a red light and was even carrying a handgun able to shoot small pellets at targets.

It was a beautiful toy.

The trouble began when his father wanted to know where he got it from.

He had to take it back to the shop apologizing for taking it although no one explained how he managed to get it out of the shop.

Apologizing to a stupis.

His father made a very big thing about it. It was wrong to take
something that did not belong to you.

It was wrong to want something you did not work for, you did
not deserve.

It was wrong to use your talent to cause harm to people.

Even to stupis.

Yes, his father knew that many of the stupis were stealing
things but that did not make it right.

The main difference between the stupis and them was that
the psi persons acted correctly because they felt that it was
the right thing to do and not just for the fear of being caught, like
the stupis.

They needed the law to control their behaviour.

A psi person should always do the right thing just because it is
right.

So Robert was a good boy, which was not easy when you
were made to practice your talent every day, a talent which
had very little practical use in everyday life,

Robert understood well the need to keep his telekinesis
hidden, but sometimes the temptation was just too strong.
Especially around Alex.

He was the school's bully, and whose mental capacity was
too low even for a stupis.

He balanced this out with size and muscle, having plenty of
both.

And a nasty temper to boot.

He got away with a lot, being one of the teacher's son,
although still had real difficulty passing his grades.

Robert was well built but like most of the psi people, was not
fond of physical activities so he lacked in the muscle
department and as such, was the perfect target for Alex.He made
Robert's life at school quite miserable until his father

taught him how to handle the situation.

In reality it was very simple.

Every time Alex threatened him, Robert just squeezed his bowels with a mental hand.

Alex learned very fast to leave him alone as every time he approached Robert, he got a bad stomach pain.

He of course did not understand what was happening , but after a while he avoided Robert as in his mind Robert became associated with pain.

For some time Robert was still having fun by doing pranks to Alex, just to pay him back.

Like when they were in the dining room, and he moved his drink close to his elbow so with his next movement Alex would knock it over.

Or by very carefully directing his fork while he was eating so he kept putting the food on his nose.

After a while Robert became ashamed of what he was doing and left him in peace. It was not fair to treat a stupis like that. Even if it was Alex.

The house was slowly getting full of people with a lot of kids and most of their parents.

His father used the opportunity of Robert's birthday to have their meeting, and while the adults retired to discuss politics the kids were left alone to do whatever they wanted.

Everybody was happy with this arrangement.

Especially the children who normally had very limited opportunities to use their talents openly.

Robert was levitating small object high into the air and Oscar was hitting them with balls of fire. The exploding objects appeared to be fireworks from the distance.

Eric, who was also telekinetic, moved the air across trying to blow the fireballs away by pushing air across their path and thus cause them to miss their target, succeeding a few times. Little Suzy, who was able to control the weight of the objects, made them move more erratically, to make it harder for Oscar to hit them.

All the children were taking a very active and very noisy part in the game, except Angelina.She was observing everything with vivid interest, but as usual for her, retiring alone in one corner.

Psi kids were much better in controlling their emotional projecting, so she felt much better in their company, still, the habit of protecting herself from unwanted feelings made her avoid close contact with people.

The really disturbing feelings could have come from the adults inside the house, but an adult psi was able to control his or her mental activity and nothing came through the closed door, in spite of the very heated discussions that went on in there.

They discussed which candidates were more suitable for Congress at the next elections, which ones would be better for their cause.

The future of the world was discussed in that room. First, this part of it, and then the rest.

....

-"But it is not fair, dad."

"Oscar, no one said that things were fair around here."

"Why should they..."

"Son, put yourself in their shoes. What would you do in their place?"

"I would not deny the right to live to a group of people just because they were different."

"They are not doing that."

"What do you mean? Then why do we have to..."

"How can they deny our right to live if they do not even know that we exist?"

"They persecuted every one of the psi individuals that happened to come out to the open. Most of them died a violent death."

"Those things happened a long time ago. People were more ignorant, more superstitious then."

"Do you think people have changed since then?"

"No. Not really deep down. People are still afraid of the unknown."

"And of something that threatens them by being better."

"Better yes, but there is nothing there you should be proud of."

"Not be proud of being better?""Son, you are coming from the same stock as all of them. The
only difference between you and them is your psychokinetic talent, which is not your achievement. It is the result of a blind genetic accident at your conception, so there is no achievement to be proud of."

"You have always said that Psi Man was a forward step on the evolutionary pathway and Homo Sapiens will disappear, just as all specimens in the past that failed to progress."

"Yes, it will happen. It is inevitable. It is the natural law of survival of the fittest. Still, that does not help us now, as it will take many generations for the natural selection to work its way."

"So we are back to square one. To shut my mouth and hide my talent."

"Yes, at least for now."

"And for many generations ahead?"

"No. That is what the pacifists amongst us believe. They want to merge with the stupis and wait for time to work."

"And is that what is going to happen?"

"No. Definitely not. A large portion of the psi population wants to be accepted in the open now. Still during this generation."

"By open war? We are stronger. We could win."

"Yes, we could win, but what then. We could not run the world without them. Our number is far too small for that."

"So, then back to square one."

"No. We have to do it the legal way. Our people are already infiltrating the key positions in politics, the armed forces, finance, religion. Very soon we will be in a position to influence the public thinking."

"I cannot see everyone simply accepting the changes needed. There will have to be people who will resist."

"Yes, there probably will be a transitory period of violence. We can handle that."

'What is the difference between that and an open war now?"

"A lot. We would be not fighting against the governments of the world. We would be the government fighting against a group of rebels. The majority would be always on our side."

"It doesn't sound very much like the Prophecy."

"Come on Oscar, you don't believe in that thing, do you?"

"A lot of people I know believe in the Prophecy. It has a very precise description of what is supposed to happen in the future and it originated from much before Nostradamus."

"Not a single intelligent person believes in prophecies today."

"But let's suppose it is true. That this psi man with some absolutely powerful talent appears and soothes the way between the psis and stupis. I even heard stories that this person already exist."

"Not the man of the Prophecy. There is a psi child who really has some potentially fantastic capacities, but that is all."

"And where is this child?"

"I don't know. All I know is that the Pacifist group has him hidden."

"Why would they hide him? I know that they are actually not our friends..."

"Not our friends? They are our enemies."

"I thought that the stupis were our enemies."

"The stupis are just pawns in the game. They have no voice in choosing the future. The Pacifists are the ones who are trying to stop us.""So what about that child?"

"He is actually a boy about your age. No one really believes that he is the Prophet but he has enormous publicity potential in our politics. His presence increases the fight between our two fractions."

"Actual fights?"

"Yes, there have been some minor physical confrontations, and they will probably increase in the future."

"But why is he so important?"

"If you believe that he is the Prophet then he is very important and as the stories say he is stupis friendly. His existence is very bad for us. He could grow up to be a very powerful leader on the Pacifist's side."

"What is so special about him?"

"I really do not know the extent of his talent. The rumours are that the Pacifist group got him through a specially designed breeding program and his education started far before he was born."

"That alone makes him special?"

"Probably not, but for political reasons it is very important for us to prevent him from growing up to be the leader of the Pacifists."

....

Angelina was having a good day.

Not a quiet day, a good day.

A good day because it was Saturday, no school today.

That meant that she was having the day away from the crowds, the intruding emotions of the people around her.
Not a quiet day as she went with Oscar and his friends to the playground.
There were a lot of children in this group but they were all psi children. They controlled their
mental projections and Angelina did not have to be constantly on guard.
Oscar did not mix with stupis children and although Angelina did not like his degrading attitude towards stupis, she looked 2forward to his company as she found peacefulness and quietness of mind with him.
There were very few places where she could let her mental barriers down and relax.
When they were on the playground the stupis children avoided it as they learned by experience that nasty things can happen if they tried to mix with this group.
So they had the playground all to themselves.
They could use their talents now, they just had to be careful not to be noticeable from a distance.
The telekinetics were showing off doing tricks with the swings which were flying around without anyone pushing them.
Oscar was proud of his trick of burning glass marbles out of the sand. Not even his father could understand how he could make clear glass out of that dirty sand.
There was a good deal of shouting, climbing and running around.
Angelina enjoyed the day in her usual way, sitting alone somewhat apart from them, capturing snippets of happy excitement escaping their control now and then.
She was the first one to notice the approaching police car with the unshielded mind of the driver, quite angry for having to

pass this way.

Still, the policeman was all smiles when he got out of the car and approached Robert,

"Your father told me to pass this way a few times to keep an eye on you. Is everything okay?"

"Yes, thank you officer, everything is fine. We are just having a bit of fun."

"Well then, I will see you later."

The smile disappeared from his face the moment he turned around towards his car.

Angelina was not very happy about the waves of emotion he sent towards her. She also very much disliked the "he is just a stupis" coming from Oscar.

She thought to send him a displeased resonance but her attention was distracted by the questioning mind coming from up the tree next to her.

The little red squirrel had a dilemma watching the sandwich in her hand. It's obvious hunger was fighting with the fear of humans based on bad past experiences.

Angelina broke off a piece of bread and put it on the ground, as far from her as she could reach without getting up. Concentrating on the little furry animal she sent it waves of calmness and reassurance.

The squirrel was visibly relaxing and in its mind Angelina appeared less and less threatening, more and more friendly. Very slowly, keeping its eyes constantly on her, the squirrel came down from the tree and with a bit of hesitation approached the piece of bread offered. Then with a quick jump grabbed the food and in the next second it was back on the tree.

While the squirrel was eating its mind radiated a deep satisfaction, a feeling of pride for his brave act and also a hint of gratitude towards Angelina.

The next moment it disappeared behind the thick branches fleeing from the big black raven sent by one of the children. Angelina was upset about the disturbance of her playing with the squirrel and sent a wave of hot itch to the boy responsible. The raven flew away as his concentration was interrupted and the boy came running towards Angelina shouting and waving his fist.

Robert had to interfere to calm the emotions down on both sides.

Robert was the accepted leader of the group, partly because he was older, and partly because he was the son of the Chief of Police, a situation which had been often beneficial to the group.

The police was less strict with them when they were a bit noisier or ran across the street.

Some of them even got a ride in a real police car with the sirens on.

Angelina always tried to avoid them. They obviously disliked having to be nice to the son of the Chief of Police and she was really upset about seeing the smiling faces and feeling the dark thoughts on the inside.

And the worst part of it was that Robert behaved the same way towards them.

Towards stupis in general.

Angelina decided to have a talk with him, to try to change his attitude.

It was not nice. All right, they were stupis, but they were also human beings.

"I definitely will have to talk to him."

Robert was also having fun.

He did not run around the playground like the other kids.

He was sitting on a swing.

He loved swings.

He tried to imitate the movements one made to make the swing move, so it would look alright from a distance, but in reality the swing was pushed by Robert's telekinetic mind.

The swing was flying with the boy clutching the chains, with his eyes closed enjoying the effortless sensation.

Robert knew that there were telekinetic people who were able to levitate themselves and actually fly.

This was his dream, to fly, to defy gravity, but he was never able to achieve it.

No one in his family had that kind of talent.

And not for lack of trying.

Robert put a lot of effort trying to train himself to levitate. His tutors were helping him but it just did not work.

He just did not have that kind of talent.

That was the problem with talents. You were either born with it or you just did not have it.

There were a lot of ways to develop a talent, to increase its potency and control but there was no way to actually create one.

So this was the closest he got to flying.

The swings.

With his eyes closed, helped by the physical sensation of his body going up and down, in his mind he could picture the playground and the other children left behind, down on the ground while he was soaring up...

It was flying.

Well, nearly.

Sooner or later he had to open his eyes and see that gravity still had a hold on him.

Every time this happened it was like waking up from a

beautiful dream into a bad reality.

It was a very bad feeling.

At times like this he sought Angelina for help and while he was crying she just took his hands and from deep inside she sent him waves of peacefulness, of wellbeing.

Very shortly he was again running, shouting with the other kids, feeling the innocent happiness what all children should feel.

....

"Thank you for coming on such a short notice. I am sorry to disturb you, but we have a couple of very important issues to discuss. "

There were five men and three women sitting around the large conference table facing the Chief of Police.

" I am getting right to the point so you can go back to your work as soon as possible.You all know that we failed in our project to elect Peter Toledo

to the Senate. This will markedly limit our activities in local politics. "

"I do not understand what happened."-The tall, grey haired woman interrupted.-"We had everything arranged..."

"Yes Thelma, we did. I do not quite understand it myself. Some of the people, actually quite a lot of them, appeared to change their mind in the last minute, and voted accordingly."

"Do you think the Pacifists had something to do with that?" – The man sitting next to Thelma appeared very calm although his white knuckles denied this appearance.

"That is a good question Tom. They probably did but there is no way to prove it."

"To cause that wide spread mental influence you would have to be very powerful. I did not think the Pacifists had that kind of power."

"Yes, they have the power. They have some very competent operators amongst them. Just remember what happened to Zacharias. He was our best Mentat and still he was wipedclean."

"I did not know that you could do that to a Mentat."

"Neither did I, but it obviously happened."-The tall dark skinned man had difficulty in controlling his emotions which still came through as he spoke.

-"What happened to Zacharias was an obvious act of violence against us. Are we going to tolerate this act of war without doing anything about it?"

"We can do nothing about it officially. As soon as it happened Steven contacted me explaining the situation. Zacharias acted outside the Code of Conduct. They had the right to defend themselves."

"Steven is Magda's offsider. That means that the child was involved."

'Yes Zoltan. Zacharias reported that he has found the child just before he was cut off."

"That child again. He comes up somewhere in the conversation, whatever we are talking about. Can we do something about him?""I can understand your anger Thelma, but it is a very difficult situation. We are also limited by the Code of Conduct and any open aggression would bring both sides against us. We can not afford that."

"We cannot afford having that child around either."

"Are you worried about the Prophecy, Thelma?"

"No. Personally I do not accept the Prophecy as relevant for this age, but there are a lot of people on both sides who are taking him seriously. If he gets to leadership he will have a very significant number of followers from both groups. This means power, and the Pacifists know that. That is why he is protected so much."

"So, what do you suggest?"

"I am not sure. Some of us, like Tom here, firmly believe that we should start open hostilities, beginning immediately."

"Hostility against the Pacifists or hostility against the stupis?"

"The Pacifists first. With them eliminated we would have no problem controlling the stupis."

"Did you stop considering that the Pacifists are our people? If we think about the world divided in psis and stupis, by attacking the Pacifists would be harming ourselves. How can you even consider this as a possibility Tom?"

"I have very strong feelings about this Silvio. Yes, the Pacifists are our people but I consider them as traitors to our way of life, and in any culture, traitors are eliminated."

"Those are very strong words Tom. You are entitled to your opinion as anyone else but I would appreciate if you would not voice that again. We, of the Council, have discussed this subject many times and the final agreement always has been to avoid open violence, especially against our own kind. After all, if we look at the moral aspect of it, this world still belongs to the stupis. We are the newcomers here."

"You sound just like a Pacifist. Are you sure you are on the right side?"

"I am not a Pacifist, far from it. I do not want to wait for the Natural Selection to do its slow work. I do want the changes now but I also prefer to avoid violence, if it is possible to do so.""It does not appear to be possible."

"It will be possible because we will make it happen, and yes, just like a Pacifist I want to share this world with the stupis, not to take it away from them. But I want our people to be the dominant fraction and I want it to happen now."

....

The big black cat was stretched out luxuriously on the window sill enjoying the warmth of the sunlight pouring in through the glass. The loud purring expressed the content feeling deep inside.

Suddenly it jumped up, back curving with all its hair in a point, hissing angrily.

The next second the cat's anger changed into fear, laying on its stomach with the head on the floor, ears pressed flat against its head.

Then the fear changed into peaceful lazy relaxation, the cat stretching out all its length in the sunlight and with its eyes closed expressed its happy feelings with loud purring.

Angelina watched the cat's display of changing emotions with a smile on her face.

Blackie was a perfect subject to practice her emotion control. The cat had a very perceptive mind and its physical body expressed beautifully the feelings inside.

Angelina focused on the cat again.

This time the cat will...

Nothing happened.

A frown appeared on the girl's face as she concentrated harder and harder.

Nothing again.

"Mother, is that you?"

"Yes, of course it is me. I am sorry for interrupting your practice but Blackie had enough for now. Don't you think so?"

"Sorry Mother, you are probably right. Just that I still have problems with sending emotions at a distance. Too frequently I don't get the response I wanted to project. Blackie is such a good subject to practice ..."

'I know daughter and I am happy to see you working so hard on your control but you always have to consider the wellbeing of others, the emotional stability of your receptor."

"I can't practice on my own.""I know that. You do have to increase your control but at the

same time you also have to remember that with a talent like yours comes a lot of responsibility. The only practical use of your talent is to help other people, to soothe pain and suffering. This has to be always your main objective. You do need practicing but never forget the wellbeing of your receptor."

....

Tock. Tock.

"What?"-Oscar woke up with a startle.

There was a small pebble floating in front of his window, hitting the glass again and again.

"It must be Robert, but what is he doing here so early on Sunday morning?

–The fishing.I completely forgot about going fishing. And it is seven 'o clock

already."

Flaming letters spelling out "ok" appeared in his window for Robert to see.

The pebble, as though it was just waiting for this sign, fell to the floor.

"It was about time you woke up."-Complained Robert while Oscar was sliding down the smooth tree trunk which stretched out in front of his window.

He did not have to hide, it was okay with his parents for him to go fishing, but why use the stairs when the tree was so conveniently placed there?"

"Sorry for this, I overslept."-Apologized Oscar while buttoning up his shirt. The rest of his clothes were more or less right.

"Where is your fishing gear?"

"I left it at the door last night. Just have to pick it up and we are ready to go."

"And just about time too."

"Common. I know that I am late but I also know that the fish will not go away." "That is not the point. We should be fishing by now."

"There is no big hurry. Anyway, I will catch more fish than you."

"In your dreams."

"I will, as long as you will not cheat by using your talent."

"I do not cheat."

"Of course not. And how did that big catfish just swim into your net last time? It did not even have a hook in its mouth."

"You were not supposed to notice that."

"But I did. You were cheating. You were pulling in that fish with your mind. That is not fishing."

"It is if you catch a fish."

"It is not the normal way of fishing."

"Of course, you prefer the stupis ways as usual."

"You are stupid if you think so."

"Do not call me stupis."

"I did not call you stupis. I called you stupid."

"I think you want a punch on your nose."

"I think you want a burn on your pant so your backside hangs out."

Oscar grinned at his friend. This kind of bantering was the norm practically every time they were together, so neither took it seriously. It was just a bit of fun while they were walking to their fishing spot which was not very far away. It was worth the walk.

The lake was not very big but it was deep and the green-brown water, although it looked murky, maintained a large variety of plant and animal life.

In the past they had been lucky a few times, catching quite nice fish, although Robert had the much voiced opinion that it was not luck.

One had to know how to catch fish.

This opinion was not mentioned the times they caught nothing, which was quite often, but very rarely remembered.

Before they actually could start fishing, though, they had to get down on their knees on the moist ground and dig for worms.

The digging was easy as the ground was soft, the worms were big and fat but there were not many of them around. It took some time to find them

"I wish Peter was here.'-Complained Oscar-'He could tell us where the worms are hiding, where to dig."

"Come on, No one can see what is under the ground."

"No. He cannot see the worms but he is able to sense the electrical signature of living things. He would know where the worms are."

"Can he feel any living things?"

"Apparently yes. Even some dead ones, if they were not dead too long."

"No wonder that he is so skinny."

"What do you mean?"

"Well, how much would you eat if your plate kept talking to you?"

"Don't make fun of him. I like Peter."

"Sorry, I did not mean it that way. I like him too. Still, that talent could be quite a useful one."

"Peter does not think so. He is spending a lot of time trying to shut it down."

"Why would anyone try to get rid of their talent?"

"Well, he says that it is very disturbing to be constantly aware of all living things around him. People, dogs, cats, birds, ants, -everything."

"Angelina had some similar problems."

"Yes, with emotions, but she learned to control it. Now she only picks up when she wants to."

"Why can't Peter do the same?"

"He is trying but not succeeding. –Okay, that is the last one. Robert, I think we got enough worms for today."

"About time too. Let's start the fishing. You really don't have to bother. I will catch more fish than you anyway."

'You wish."

"I bet you I will get the first fish."

"You are on. The only fish you will see today will be the ones I am catching."

Within a few minutes Robert had a big bite. His rod bent down nearly touching the water and the reel was noisily loosing line. It was a big fish. It pulled like a horse.

Even Oscar was shouting and jumping around.

Still, all that excitement did not last long. The pulling suddenly stopped and the line was dead in the water.

"You lost it." –Oscar was not sure if he should be upset for losing such a good fish or if he should be happy about the fact that Robert did not get the first fish.

It should be his turn now.

But, it was not, it wasn't anyone's turn.

The fishing lines were undisturbed in the water and every now and again when they pulled the lines in to check them, the baits were still on the hook. Untouched.

"It looks like that was the only fish in the water."

"Sure. It is all your fault." –Robert exploded- "You had to be so loud when I hooked that fish. You frightened all the others away."

"I got a bit excited. It was a big fish."

"You are still too loud. You act as if you have never fished before."

"Cut it out. You know that I have beaten you quite a few times. Okay, okay. You have beaten me too, but that is not the point. I don't think that the sound of my voice could cause much disturbance under the water."

"So where is all the fish?" "They probably just don't like you."

"I can't see you catching anything. Besides, you are still shouting."

"This is not shouting."

"You are still disturbing the fish."

"Sure. Next time I will use mind speech to talk to you. Would that make you happy?"

"Some people are able to do just that, you know."

"I wish I could."

"Mind speech?"

'Yes. Direct mind to mind communication."

"I know what it is. We have a kid at school able to do it. He can't use it, mind you."

"Why not?"

"You need two people to mind speak. One who is able to project their thoughts and another who is able to receive them."

"So why can't he mind talk at school?"

"Because there is no one else at school that is able to. He probably knows people he can use his talent with, but not at school."

"I heard that any psi person could learn mind speech to some degree. I believe it is a capacity linked to your talent."

"Yes, I know. My parents can mind speak. They wanted me to

learn too, but it is too much work. They agreed that I should
start training after finishing school. Miss Strudy at schooltold me
once that they are planning to introduce it as a
separate subject. Mind speech."

"Nice. I am not looking forward to having another difficult
subject to study. I have enough trouble as it is."

"Come on Oscar, you have no problems at school."

"Well, in an ordinary school I would probably be great., but we
go to a school for psi kids. I struggle sometimes."

"To tell you the truth, I prefer fishing too."

"I like fishing too; still I would like to catch something."

"It would be nice. Except that big pull at the beginning, nothing
seems to be happening. It is like,,,,Hey! Look at that. What is
it?"

Not very far from them a row of vertical sticks appeared to
travel on the surface of the water.

"It's the dorsal fin of something big moving just under the
surface. Quick, use your talent Robert. Bring it closer."

"No way. You've already accused me of cheating today."

"I don't want to catch it. I just want to have a closer look at it. It
seems huge."

The fish appeared to struggle with something for a short time,
then half lifted above the surface of the water and started to
drift towards the boys.

It was getting nearer and nearer, struggling all the time trying
to get away, but Robert had a strong mental hold on it .

It was a beautiful fish.

Bright yellow-green on its side, a deep dark green on its back.

"It is a carp, A big one."- Declared Oscar reaching out to touch
the fish which was at their feet by then.

The fish made a big splash with its tail and disappeared back
into deep water.

"You let it go."

"You said that you only wanted to look at it. You did that."

"It was a big fish."

"It was that. A nice one."

"So why did you let it go?"

"You want to accuse me of cheating again?"

"No. You are right. Still, we won't catch a fish like that again."

....

Angelina dropped the book she was reading on the floor.
Pressing both hands against her forehead she tried to push
out the sudden, intense pain.

The strong wave of anger was like a knife cutting into her
brain.

Then just as suddenly as it came it disappeared, leaving her
shaking in her seat.

What a strong emotion.

It must have been a very powerful mind that sent it and the
sudden cut off was probably due to a strong control.

It must have been a momentary slip of control due to the
strong emotion, control which was then regained, fast.

But what a power.

"Who are you?"

Angelina had been practicing with Peter, whose natural talent
was telepathy. He was teaching her how to concentrate and
send thoughts out.

She had no natural talent for mind speech but was trying very
hard to learn it.

Sometimes, but only sometimes, they were actually able to
communicate with each other at a distance.

"Who are you?" – Angelina sent a questing wave out –"Who
are you out there?"

There was no answer.

That powerful mind was closed to outside enquiries.
Such a powerful mind.
Angelina felt certain it was a young mind.
A very young mind.
The anger was directed against a school.
It must have been a schoolboy.
But what power.
The encounter left her weak for the rest of the day.

....

CHAPTER FIVE

Angelina still had not recovered completely by the following
morning when she received the urgent call from Peter.

The mental message was clear.

There was some problem with Alicia and they needed her
help.

Alicia was a strange little girl. She was seven years old but
looked like four.

A very small, thin girl who would have looked pretty with those
big blue eyes and blonde hair, but her appearance was
spoiled by her pale, very white skin and a constantly serious
expression on her face.

She did not appear to have any psi talent but everyone felt
depressed in her company.

She appeared to radiate a feeling of penetrating gloom.

Her parents were well respected in the psi society, but not
very much liked.

They did not appear to have any friends, they did not
participate in any activity within the psi community.

Oscar once overheard his father say that he had goose
bumps whenever he passed near them.

He called them Dark Psis and did not want to talk about them
when Oscar asked what that meant.

He just said that some people had the capacity to call up
energies not quite belonging to this world.

On arriving at the playground, Angelina found Alicia sitting on
the ground, hugging her knees, rocking back and forth.

She saw Peter as well as a few other kids, surrounding Alicia,
obviously trying to calm her down, she could feel the intense
fear emanating from Alicia from quite some distance, and
understood why Peter had called her.

As soon as she got to her, she cupped the girl's head in her hands, and sent her soothing waves of calmness and wellbeing from deep inside herself.

Alicia was visibly relaxing and in a very short time, stopped rocking and was quietly sobbing on Angelina's shoulder.

"What happened Peter?"- Angelina kept hugging the girl to herself.

"I am not sure. She said something about a black animal with large eyes and big teeth but when I arrived I didn't see anything."

"Did you try to read her?"

"I did and I got out very fast too. I nearly panicked myself."

"What do you mean?"

"She has a strange mind. Dark and menacing. I got out very fast."

"She was panicking. That was what you picked up."

"No, I could have dealt with that. Her basic mind structure is strange, frightening. I have never felt anything like that."

"So she is definitely psi, but we still don't know what her talent is."

"I am not sure I want to find out."

By this time the little girl was quiet, but still holding on to Angelina for comfort.

"Come on Alicia, tell me what happened."

It took a while until the girl was able to talk.

"It was a big, nasty magpie. It kept attacking me. Pinching my head and back, again and again. It was hurting me. I was afraid."

"What did you do?"

"I was alone."

"I know, but you must have done something. What happened?"

"I was very afraid. I called for help."

"Who did you call?"

"I am not sure. There was no one around. I just called."

"Then what happened?"

Alicia buried her face in Angelina's shoulder.

"That big thing ate the magpie."

"What big thing?"

The rest of the story was very difficult to get out of her. The poor girl needed Angelina's soothing to stop her from panicking again.

Eventually, though, they managed to get some sort of story out of her.

Apparently when she sent out that call for help, a large hole opened in the ground in front of her.

A large, black thing came out of that hole, with big eyes and huge teeth, lunged at and ate the bird attacking her.

It then, after having a very close look at the panicking girl, went back into the hole, which then closed behind it.

Peter and Angelina just looked at each other, not quite knowing what to think of the story.

The only thing they could do now was to take the girl back to her parents.

They surely would know what to do with her.

The parents were happy to see them.

"I am very glad that Alicia has such good friends. Thank you for your help."- The girl 's father shook their hands.

Peter did not want to leave it at that.

"Excuse me sir, but could you please explain what exactly happened here? We are both very confused."

"Gladly, but it is not very simple to explain. Alicia has a special talent which runs in our family. It usually manifests itself when one is much older, but it appears that the fright caused by that bird brought it to the surface earlier than expected. She could not handle it as she's had no special training for it as yet."

"And what is her talent? What can she do?"

"Well, it would take a lot of time to fully explain, but she is, or at least she will be, able to call on energies and contact entities not quite belonging to this world as we know it."

....

The playground was unusually quiet.

Not because it was empty, because it was not.

There were quite a few children there, sitting on the ground around the swings.

Sitting and talking quietly.

This might sound unnatural for this age group, but these were not any kind of children.

They were psi children.

Children who were growing up with strict mind training in order to achieve full control of their talent.

Children who knew when to play and when to be quiet.

Alicia was not amongst them although she was the main subject of their conversation.

By now every one of them knew what happened on that playground the day before.

"It could have been just her imagination. No one actually saw it happen."

"Her parents confirmed that she is able to do what she said."

"What happened exactly? Peter, you were the first to arrive, what did you see?"

"I was the first one there because her mental scream nearly knocked me off my chair, and I was a few blocks away."

"But what did you actually see?"

"The same as everyone else. A very frightened girl and a few feathers on the floor."

"That is not a lot of information."

"No. It is not. Does anyone know more about it? What about you Robert? I know that you have been talking to your father about what happened."

"I didn't get much out of him. He just said that the Dark Psis are very powerful people with very dangerous talents. All I could get out of him was that sometimes in the past some of them miss-used their talents causing a lot of harm to a lot of people.
Because of this past they are not liked very much, and are avoided."

"I do not know about you Robert, but this gives me more questions than answers. What about you Oscar? Was your father more helpful?"

"Yes, he was. Apparently he has an acquaintance who has a dark talent. He was assisting police investigations in a very unusual way."

"Good. Tell us more. As far as I am concerned, I have never heard of dark talents before. I know nothing about them."

"I am not sure I do."

"But your father explained it to you."

"Yes, he did, and made it very simple. Well, simple for him. I did not get half of what he said."

"Well?"

"Okay, okay. But remember that you are making me explain something I do not understand myself."

"Fine. Just tell us what your father said.""Okay. Well, he started to talk about us. That we, with our
talents, control different aspects of our environment. We are able to control fire, water, gravity, time flow and such, we influence our world, the world which is around us."

"That is obvious."

"But also there are psi people who have talents capable of reaching out and influencing things in other environments, in other worlds."

"You mean on another planet?"

"No, this one. Our planet, but a different world. A place which... I don't know. It is too complicated to explain."

"What else did your father say?"

"Well, he tried to explain by using our house as an example. He said that we are all living in the same house, my parents and I, me in my room and they in theirs. My room is my world and when I have my door closed, I am not aware of their world, even if I know that it is there.

He said that right here, where we are now there is another world. We just do not see it as the door is closed."

"I think you've just complicated things for me. What else did your father say?"

"Not much more, except that manipulating our environment as we are doing can't do much harm, but bringing in new energies or living things to an environment they do not belong to, could be very dangerous."

"Why? We have enough strange things around as it is, and they do not seem to do much harm."

"Remember that fish Mrs Marks was talking about at school? The one which was brought into our river probably by accident? It did not belong to this environment, had no natural enemies. It went out of control and created havoc amongst the local fish."

"What has that got to do with..?"

"There are lots of unexplained cases in the history books describing unusual forces or beings causing much harm. A lot of psi persons were called witches and burned to death because of that."

"You mean that the witches and the demons in the movies are all real?" – The shaky voice belonged to Gloria, a tiny seven year old girl who went to the same class as the twelve year olds because of her high IQ.

"Not quite. Not the ones in the movies, but they are probably based on some real occurrences."

....

"My son Robert asked me about the Dark Talents."

The two men were sitting comfortably in the Chief of Police's dining room. The comfortable chairs, the drinks in their hands or the warm after dinner glow could not cover the sudden tension in the room.

"What did you tell him?"

"Very little. I really did not know how to approach the subject."

"You had several alternatives."

"Yes, I know. One of them would be the popular spirit/demon explanation. I did not want to go that way."

"You could have told him the real version."

"Yes, perhaps I should have. But how do you explain alternate realities to a child?"

"Do not underestimate Robert. He is a smart child."

"It is not him. It is me. I myself have difficulties in accepting those theories."

"They are not theories."

"You don't really know that."

"Come on Anton. We all know about their talents."

"Really? Do you really understand your own talent? You have a pyrokinetic family. Do you really understand how and why your talent works?"

"I've got full control of my talent."

"And I can drive a car without understanding anything about its mechanics."

"It is not quite the same."

"Probably not. Still, I do not know how I defy gravity. I can do it, I can move, I can lift things without touching them physically, but deep down at the energy level I do not know what is happening. And I understand far less anything about the Dark Talents."

"I never liked that name."

"It is just a historical stigmata, but it expresses the vast differences between our Talent and theirs"

"My son, Oscar, asked me the same question. I tried to answer the best I could."

"A few other people I know made the same comment. Their children asking questions. What is happening? Why is this sudden interest in Dark Talents?"

"Apparently they all witnessed an apparition."

"That episode with Alicia? What did actually happen?"

'Well yes, it was probably what stirred them up. They did not actually see the happening, just found the frightened girl right after it happened. As she is underage for her talent, she's had no training at all as yet. When that bird frightened her, she instinctively called on her Talent for help and the apparition that responded to her call frightened her even more.

Then when the kids found her, she told them the story."

"Why hasn't she been trained?

"I am not sure. They have their own ways to prepare their child."

"So, what should we do now?"

"About what? About the children or about the Dark Psis?"

"About the children. I do not think the questions will stop. Not much we can do about the Dark Talents."

"Why should we do anything about them? Although they keep

very much to themselves, they are our allies. They could be
very useful in the near future."

'The Dark Talents? Useful? That would be a first."

"Do not underestimate them. They control forces of
tremendous power."

"So what?"

"Remember our work. Very soon we might have to oppose the
Pacifists in an open confrontation. Magda and her group
represent powers we dare not face without the help of
the Dark Ones."

....

The air appeared clear but there was a strong, eye watering
stench in the room, like burning rubber.

The big, dog like thing was peacefully lying on the carpet
looking at them with those huge yellow eyes. In spite of its
peaceful appearance, those large white teeth hanging out
from both sides of its snout even when it was closed, did not
invite a friendly approach.

"This was what I called for help?" – Alicia's voice was quite
shaky remembering their previous encounter.

'Maybe not this exact one but one of the same kind."

"What are they?"

"Well, it is hard to define. We call them angor, which is just a
name, it does not mean anything. They are similar to our dogs
but far more intelligent. They are very docile and friendly
when they feel controlled, but could be very destructive on
their own."

"What is this smell?"

"I really don't know. It must be something in the air from
where they come from.

Every being from there arrives with the same smell but when the air clears, they themselves do not appear to smell."

"Every being? Are there others?"

"Of course. Their world is full of life. All types and shapes. Some of them are quite intelligent, they have a language, and appear to have an organized civilization."

"And you have seen them all, Dad?"

"Maybe not all but a lot of them."

"And they come any time you call them?"

"Well, yes. Kind of."

"What do you mean, kind of?"

"When I call them they have to come. I can control them but they don't like to be forced. Specially the more intelligent ones. They could be quite nasty."

"Nasty?"

"Yes. Most of them try to attack me or at least try to escape."

"Then why do you call them if you know that they will try to harm you?"

"I very rarely call them. Only when I really need their help, and even then I try to give them something in exchange for their service. Anyway, they can't harm me as I am fully in control of them."

"What would happen if they escaped your control?"

"Well, use your imagination. They are on a strange world, they are very powerful and very angry."

"Not a nice thought. Has it ever happened?"

"Not to me, but yes, it has happened. Mostly to people who were in training and accidentally called on an entity they could not control. This is why you should never practice your Talent alone. You always need someone fully trained present."

"It looks like I was very lucky at the playground."

"Yes, you were. You were lucky that an angor answered your

call, one which was not hungry, and one which probably was doing something pleasurable when you called, so it was happy to just go back."

"It sounds worse than what I thought it was."

"Yes, and it would have been my fault for not training you. I did not anticipate this early arrival of your Talent, it had never happened before. I'd better talk to the others to change our training schedules. We got lucky this time but cannot afford to let it happen again."

....

"Leave me alone."

The playground was nearly empty now, only a small group of children were sitting on the floor next to the swings.

Alice was again the centre of attention but this time she was there.

"Common Alicia, we are your friends."

"If you were my friends you would leave me alone. And you, Angelina, get out of my mind."

"I only wanted to make you feel better."

"I know that but I do not like to be manipulated, not even by you."

"You should not talk to Angelina like that" - Peter was defending his friend.-"She only wanted to help you."

"I am sorry Angelina, I just want to be left alone."

"We are friends. We form a group. We help each other. We discuss our problems together. We always had."

"I don't have any problems, Peter."

"That is not true. You have changed since the incident that happened here last time. You behave differently. We are here to help you and we expect you to help us."

"Me ,help you?"

"Yes. We witnessed something here that we would like to

understand. You could help us."

"There is nothing to understand. It was an uncontrolled manifestation of my Talent. It's unexpected, early appearance unbalanced me emotionally and I found it difficult to cope, but I am doing okay now. You can't help me. I just need time and training."

"I can understand that, and we can leave you alone if that is what you want, but remember, we are always here for you."

"Thank you."

"Which does not change our wish to learn more about your Talent."

"You can't learn my Talent."

"I am aware of that. You have to be born with a Talent. Still, we would like to understand it."

"What do you want to know?"

"Well, you know about our Talents. We manipulate different aspects of our environment. Whatever we do, affects only our immediate surroundings. You do something different. What is it that you are actually doing?"

"It is fairly simple. It is like when Peter sent me that mental message to come here to the playground. I received the message and came here. We do the same thing. We send out a message and things respond."

"What things?"

"The things we call."

"Where are these things?"

"Now, that is the part which is hard to explain."

"Try. We have some intelligence."

"It is not that. Do you know about alternate realities?"

"Well, my father recently explained that to me, which does not mean that I understood any of it."

"That is just it. At this stage of my training I don't understand it either."

"Well, if it is a part of understanding your Talent, tell us what you know."

"I've got a kind of explanation in my head, though I am not sure if it is the right one. Still, it helps me to organize things in my mind."

"Let's hear it."

"The basic concept is very simple. Our reality, which includes us, the air, the sunshine, the buildings, and everything else around us, is not the only one. In the same physical space, there are other realities, with other people, other lives, other solar systems, all different from ours and not in contact with each other."

"How can you have two different things in the same physical space?"

"That is the crunch of it. The way I explain it, and I am not sure that it is the right explanation, is using waves. Different waves, like you can have several sound or magnetic waves in the same physical space, as each one of these transmit independently. You can send electrical discharges of different frequency along the same wire , at the same time. Something like that is happening with the different realities."

"Realities? How many of them are there?"

"I do not know how many, but quite a few."

"How can you know that?"

"My father told me that sometimes he called on several intelligent beings at the same time and they did not recognize each other."

"And you are able to contact them?"

"Yes, that is our Talent. Sometimes we are able to cross mentally the barriers between realities and control the beings on the other side."

"Control?"

"Yes. You have to. It would be very dangerous bringing something you do not control into this reality."

....

"Did you call me, dad?"

Alicia's voice was a bit hesitant. Her father had never before called her this late after her bedtime.

"Yes, Alicia, please come in. I would like to talk to you."

Besides her father there were two very old, elegantly dressed men sitting around the big table.

"Am I in trouble?"

"No, not this time."-Her father laughed, trying to lighten the situation.

-"Please sit down."

Now Alicia was really worried.

Her father always kept his business affairs very separate from his family life. She had never before been invited to adult company.

"These two gentlemen are senior members of our Council. Their presence here should indicate the seriousness of the situation. I'll come straight to the point Alicia. We have a potentially serious problem in our hands, and we are not very sure what to do about it. We just had a long discussion and the only suitable solution we can find to the problem involves you."

'Me?"

"Yes. Remember the angor you summoned at the playground? It was not just friendly to you, it really liked you. For some strange reason you two established a mental bond which still persists through the barrier which separates our worlds."

"I can't see a problem with that."

"The problem is that the angor is really looking for ways to get back to you and thanks to that bond it just might be able to do it."
"I still can't see the problem."
"It is a big problem. You do not want an uncontrolled angor loose in this world.
Besides, if it manages to get through the barrier, other creatures might use the same breach to get through."
"Might?"
"Yes, might. This situation never presented itself before so we really don't know what might or might not happen."
"So, break the bond."
"You can't just break a mental bond. Only by eliminating at least one of the protagonists can a mental block be terminated."
"You mean killing the angor or killing me. I do not like either of the solutions. Isn't there any other way?"
"Yes, there are other alternatives, but eliminating the angor would be the easier one.""I really would not like to do that. Are there any other
alternatives?"
"An other way would be to close your Talent. That would break the bond."
"I did not know that you can close a Talent for a while."
"No. Not for a while. It is only possible to close it permanently."
"I certainly would not like that. Any other way? So far I do not like any of your solutions."
"There is only one other way. And that is to bring both participants of the bond to the same side of the barrier."
"You mean..?"
"Yes Alicia. And it will put a lot of responsibility on your shoulders."

"I always wanted a big dog."

....

"Come on, Puppy. Stop moving around. I am trying to sleep."
The big dog-thing was stretched out on the floor, with its large
head resting on its paws, it swung its head around, to watch
the little girl getting comfortable, digging herself into the long,
black fur on the beast's side until only her face was showing.
The fur was very long and incredibly soft and the warm body
of the animal made it very comfortable and cosy.
Alicia felt warm and safe in there.
The huge eyes watching her and the very large, curved teeth
hanging out at each side of the long snout did not appear to
bother her.
She liked this angor.
She trusted it as a friend.
Although her father warned her several times not to release
her control over the animal under any circumstances, she kind
of kept forgetting about it.
She accepted her father's reasons that the animal was an
unknown entity that you could never be sure what it would do
if allowed to roam free, she also felt that there was a special
bond between her and the angor, a kind of friendship, and the
behaviour of the animal appeared to confirm this.
It had to be really forced to separate from her, and when they
were together it discouraged other people from approaching
them.
It was not really aggressive or anything like that, but when
someone talked to Alicia, there was a lot more teeth showing,
which was quite enough to keep most people away.
Besides being a wonderful, protective pet for Alicia, the angor
was very useful in other ways too.
It was perfect for Alicia to practice the control of her Talent

and to get an insight into the workings of the alien mind. The angor was a happy subject, readily participating in her training sessions, even appeared to be enjoying them.

Her father also noticed this bond between the two, but did not trust the angor as much as his daughter did.

He made sure that, the angor was under constant mental supervision all the time, day or night by a well-trained Dark Talent.

Not interfering but ready to do so if ever it was required.

It was never required.

Those large eyes appeared to observe everything with an unusual intelligence for an animal.

In a very short time it learned the meaning of the words used around it and also learned the rules to follow when living together with humans. Both of these were very alien to the world it came from.

Alicia was nearly sure that it was able to follow the conversations of people around them.

She used long words and complicated phrases purposely when talking or giving commands and the angor always responded the appropriate way.

The only problem was that they were restricted to home. She could not really take the angor on a leash out to the streets.

It was not a very tough restriction as they had a large garden area with an eight foot fence all around it to keep the animal in.

The fence, by the way, just appeared overnight, thanks to the helpers her father called upon with his Talent.

It was quite a nice fence but not very effective as demonstrated one afternoon, when Alicia and Robert were in the yard playing with a ball, and Robert accidentally kicked the ball over the fence. The angor just jumped over the fence and came back with the ball in its mouth.

Alicia kind of forgot to mention this to her father.

The angor in general liked the children.

It got along well with all of them, but always stayed close to Alicia.

The children, after they got used to the rather ferocious appearance, warmed up to it.

They touched it, pulled its fur, climbed all over it.

Oscar even invented a new game climbing up onto its head then sliding down along the back on the silky fur.

It was fun and the angor did not mind.

It did not have to be controlled; it even appeared to enjoy it.

Alice noticed that when the children were around much less of its teeth were visible.

Still, what it most appeared to like was watching people doing things.

As it was allowed to roam freely around the house it was quite common that everywhere there was some kind of activity, its head would appear in the door, and just standing or laying down there, watching, listening.

Always watching, always listening.

Watching people in the kitchen using the utensils.

Watching Alice's father using his computer and recording equipment.

Watching people interacting, listening in at their meetings.

No one minded it.

It was just a dog.

But those big eyes were intelligent. That alien mind was learning.

....

Angelina woke up suddenly from a restless sleep.

That voice again.

That mental scream of anger, frustration.

It lasted probably less than a second but its power was tremendous.

It was a very short slip of a powerful mental control caused by a sudden emotional outburst.

Someone really must have upset him.

Angelina felt sorry for the fellow towards whom that anger was directed.

A mind of that power could dish out a very serious punishment.

What Angelina was most impressed by was the sudden cut off, the sudden ceasing of that wave of emotion.

It was like a steel door slamming shut.

There was nothing left there to perceive.

Angelina concentrated, trying to pick up some slight remains of the emotion, but there was nothing there.

The shut off was complete, indicating a strong mind control.

Still, that very short burst of energy gave a lot of information to Angelina.

It was the same mind that frightened her before.

That same young school boy who had some problem with the school.

Although this time it was a bit different.

This time he was not directly involved. A person was doing harm to someone close to him. A girl.

So, he had a girlfriend and someone was trying to harm her.

Poor fellow. He should have picked an easier victim.

He would be very sorry by now.

....

"Common Peter, you are a telepath. You should be able to pick up at least traces of him."

"Yes, I should. But I don't. That gives me a reason to doubt your story."

"Do you think I am lying?"

"No. Of course not. Besides, I would pick up on that. But you could be mistaken."

"How can I be mistaken in that? I sent you the emotional burst I picked up. Was that not enough?"

"It was. Thank you. And nearly at burn-out intensity. I still have a headache."

"You said to send it to you the way I received it."

"How come the intensity didn't affect you?"

"I am used to it. I've learned to absorb emotional outbursts."

"But such power."

"Exactly. That is why I cannot understand why you couldn't pick him up. You just can't hide a person like that."

"It is unlikely, but it is possible. A mind with that kind of power can also have a strong control barrier."

"That strong?"

"Well, it must be. Otherwise I would pick him up even if he tried to hide."

"Did you analyse it?"

"Yes, but I picked up less than you did. I can't feel the emotional content as you do. I can pick up the thought patterns but it was a very short wave to do it well."

"What did you pick up?"

"Well, that he is a boy of about our age, very well trained as the sending was very regular. I also picked up some visuals. Some kind of vehicle with two men and a girl inside. The men were stupis, the girl...I am not sure. She had some connection with the boy. I could not get anything else. Oh, yes. There was also a very old woman involved, but I think she was on his side."

"Could you pick up anything else about her?"

"No, she was completely closed to me. I only picked her up as a reflection in his mind."

"Was she dressed in black?"

"She could have been. I do not know. Why?"

"I've got a strange suspicion about our boy."

....

More than two months passed since the angor established itself as part of the household.

It was an ideal pet.

Very clean when eating, completely house trained.

In spite of its large size never damaged the furniture or the multiple ornaments collected by Alicia's father over the years from all over the world.

Did not seek anyone's company, except Alicia's, but did not refuse anyone else's approach either.

Those big eyes seemed to absorb everything from everywhere.

For Alice, the angor was a terrific help.

With daily practice, the control over her Talent improved greatly and the angor did not appear to mind being put through all those test situations.

Even seemed to enjoy them.

Slowly there was a very strong bond building up between them. The big, dog-like thing was doing whatever Alice wanted it to do before she sent it the order to do it.

This would have appeared strange to anyone else, but to Alice's childish trust it felt normal.

Very soon, though, she changed her mind.

....

It was a very lazy Sunday morning.

Late in bed, no hurry for breakfast.

Alicia's parents went away the day before to a gathering of
the Dark Talents and were not due back until late that night.
The two were practically alone in the big house.
Alicia, still in bed was already missing the angor's company.
Using her Talent she extended a call.
"You do not have to order me to come to you. Just extend me
a wish and I will come."
The soft voice was like a loud alarm bell in Alicia's mind.
She sat up in bed, fully awake now, looking around.There was no
one in the room.
The angor just walked in slowly, with its head low and those
large yellow eyes fixed on her.
"Hello Puppy. For a moment I was thinking that you were
talking to me. Were you?"
Alice grinned on the absurdity of the thought.
"But, then who was it? I definitely heard someone talking to me."
"It was me."
"Who? Where are you?"
"It is me. The angor you call Puppy. Not a very dignified name
but I like it. It seems to express a kind of friendliness. I thank
you for that."
"Puppy?"
"Yes Alice, it is me."
"But...when did you learn to talk?"
"I could always talk. In my world there are a lot of people
whose mouths are not built for vocalization. We normally use
mind talk. It was you who took time to be able to listen."
"But you are talking to me."
"If you listen carefully you will notice that there is no noise in
the air, only concepts in your mind."
Alice was familiar with the concept of mind speech. Lots of
her friends, like Peter, were telepaths. She herself never

experienced it as she did not have the talent.

"But I am not a telepath."

"So how do you explain being able to hear me?"

"I don't know."

"Your people, the ones you call Dark Talent, have a freak emission wave that is able to manipulate the function of our minds. We have no defence against it. We are compelled to do whatever you are ordering us to do. So, you order us around, but never listen. You never developed the capacity to hear us."

"My father told me that we always have to maintain complete control of the beings we call across, otherwise they would do terrible things. When you are doing that, you can't listen at the same time."

"And what do you expect? You call us across against our will; you force us to work for you, then you drop us back as if nothing has happened. Do you expect us to like it?"

"We don't do that."

"No? That large fence around you property, how did it appear overnight? Did human workers do the job? Did your father pay for it?"

"My father said that he always tried to repay you for the work rendered."

"With trinkets. He does not know anything about us, how we live, what we need. The things he regularly sends back with us are not just useless but most of the time harmful to our environment."

"I am sure he does not know that."

"In what way does that help?"

"So what about you? You appeared to come over willingly. I thought you liked us. I am not controlling you now, so what are you going to do? Are you going to eat me?"

"If I had a mouth like you I would be laughing. We are not like that. Our body shapes might appear to your culture as threatening, but in reality we are quite peaceful. In our relationship you are the aggressor."

'Me?"

'Your race. You are the ones invading our world. You are the ones kidnapping us."

'We are not kidnapping anyone."

"No? Then what do you call it?"

"We ...I don't know. You make it all appear so awful, so mean."

"Because it is awful. It is very much equivalent to the slavery you are so against now, but was accepted as normal in your past."

"I did not know any of this and I don't think anyone else does, either. If it is so bad for you and it has been going on for such a long time, why didn't you do anything about it? At least you could have tried to let us know."

"We tried to communicate with your people but your minds were closed to our mind speech. The barrier is closed to us. We can't cross it to enter your world. Only the dark talent of your people can do that."

"So, if we are so nasty to your people, what are you doing here pretending to be an animal, pretending to like us?"

"I'm not just pretending to like it here. Admittedly I did at first, you being our enemy and all that, still, I felt that there was a kind of bond between us at our first encounter and I wanted to explore that further."

"There has to be more, here.. I do not believe that you are here only for a friendly visit."

"There is nothing else."

"My friend Peter once told me that you can't lie in a mind link.

Yet you are lying."

"Okay, okay. There are things I do not want to tell you but since I can only communicate with you in mind speech, you have the advantage of being able to lie while vocalizing."

'I've got nothing to hide."

"How do I know that?"

"Okay. Teach me mind speech then we will be at the same level."

"I do not need to teach you anything. Your Talent has emitting capacities, as you are able to control our mind. You can't connect with us on the same level because you've never actually tried. Try to tune down your Talent to a conversational level—Ouch—not that hard.

Tune it down more. A lot more. Okay, that's it. I am getting that you have a headache."

"Okay. So now you can see that I am not lying. Why are you?"

"I am not lying to you. Just that there are things I am not ready to tell you yet."

"What things?"

"Things."

"That is not very helpful. My father might be able to understand you better."

"If you tell your father about me, I will be dead."

"Why would he kill you?"

"If you tell him about me, my status of an innocent dog would instantly change to an unknown entity, probably a dangerous invader of your world. He could not afford the risk of leaving me alive."

"You are probably right in that. So what now? If we don't kill you, will you kill me to keep your secret?"

"You know very well that I could not do that even if I wanted to. You can control my mind at any time. Besides, in the mind link you are aware that I have no bad intentions towards you

or your people."
"I can feel that as true. So, what now?"
"Well, until I see that things are different, we can continue playing the roles of the innocent little girl and her dog, although we know that both statements are lies."
"Why is my side a lie?"
"Your mind is too mature to belong to a little girl like you."
"I am not sure how to take that."
"Take it as a compliment. It is a good thing to have a mature mind no matter how young you are."
....
"Hi, Angelina..Hey...you are getting good in this mind speech thing."
"I had a good teacher."
"Thank you, but why are you so upset?"
"I am not upset. I just got some problems. I need your advice."
"Why me? Oscar is older and much better at solving problems."
"Not the kind of problem I have."
"Okay, you got me curious. Go ahead."
"Not like this. Too many people can listen in."
"Not if you personalize the sending of...sorry we did not get that far in your training."
"So?"
"So what?"
"Are you going to help me or not?"
"Of course I will. Meet you at the playground after school."
....
"Okay, what is the big problem?"
At this late time of the day the playground was empty.
It was not dark yet but it was getting there and the two children sitting on the swing looked very young in their school

uniform.

"I am in trouble and don't know what to do.?"

"What did you do?"

"Nothing. It is not that kind of problem."

"Then what is it? Girl, you have to give me something. I've got no idea what you are talking about."

"It is a bit complicated."

"Star at the beginning."

"Okay. I'll try. You know how badly our parents want to find this so called Prophet?"

"Yes. Everybody knows that. What does that have to do with you?"

"Well, I think I know how to find him."

"That is fantastic. They will be very happy to know that. I don't know much about the politics they are involved in, but the Prophet appears to have a very important role in it."

"That is where the problem lies."

"You lost me again.'

"What do you think will happen if they find him?"

"I don't really know. I never thought about it."

"They will kill him."

"Why would they do that for? He is one of us."

"That is exactly the problem. He is not one of us. He is the future leader of the Pacifists. The group our parents plan to go against."

"So?"

"It will be war, most probably a very violent one. They cannot afford a powerful leader on the opposite side and because of the talents he is supposed to have, they are not expecting to be able to convert him."

"So? What does it have to do with you?"

"He is a child. Of our age. They want to kill a child."

"I still fail to see your involvement in their politics."

"How can I help my father to kill a child?"

'So don't tell him what you can do."

"And how can I go against my father? Not to help him in something he wants so much?"

"Oh. I see your problem now. If you help him, you feel guilty. If you do not help him, you feel guilty again."

"So what do I do?"

"I don't know, and by the way, do you realize that you have put me in the same situation? By knowing this, should I tell my father about it, or not?"

"So we've both got the same problem now."

"Thank you."

"Sorry about that, I really am."

"I still don't understand why you had to involve me in this."

"Because you could help me."

"How? By making a choice between killing a child and lying to my father?"

"No, I've got a kind of a plan."

"That doesn't sound very promising."

"Well, I am not sure, but if instead of lying to our parents by not helping them, we just postpone the telling."

"Why would that help?"

"We can first try to find this Prophet by ourselves, talk to him and then decide what to do."

"That sounds good, but how the hell are you going to find him? As far as I know the whole Council failed to do that."

"I said I might have a way."

"I am listening."

"It is a bit complicated."

"Angelina!"

"Okay, okay. I will try to explain. You know about my Talent, picking up emotions and all that."

'Who are you talking to?"

"Sorry. You know about me more than anyone else, but I need to tell you a couple of things more.

Once I learned to control my talent and achieved not to get affected by the emotions absorbed, I started a kind of mental game, most of the time just before I went to sleep.

I spread out my awareness, at a very low receptive intensity, but to a very large area, receiving emotions from hundreds of people from all around.

As it was at a very low intensity, I did not get any particular emotion but more like a general, low grade hum. As I stretched my awareness further and further out, the feeling that I received was like a large, soft, grey blanket made up by a very large number of soft emotional noises. As I spread my awareness further and further out this hum got softer and softer, until I fell asleep."

"This is probably a fantastic experience, something I could never achieve. But what has it to do with our problem?"

"Recently my blanket sometimes has holes in it."

"You have what?"

"Holes in my blanket."

"How the hell can you have holes in a blanket made up of emotional discharges?"

"I think I know how."

"Please illuminate me."

"The holes in the blanket would indicate areas from where there is no incoming mental waves."

"You mean there is no one there?"

"No, I mean there is someone there who is not sending,"

"There is no such person. You can't completely shut down mental activity. My father has a perfect control still, I can always perceive when he approaches. There is no such person."

"Except maybe one."

"No...I see what you mean. The Prophet is an unknown entity. He might be able to do it. Then the problem is solved. Follow the hole and you find the Prophet."

"Not that easy. I can feel the hole, but I am not able to localize it. Especially when I am half asleep."

"Then we are back to square one."

"Not quite. You could mentally follow my emotional spread and pinpoint the location of the hole."

....

"Come on, Puppy, what is wrong? You know, I am starting to recognize your facial expressions and you do not look happy."

"I am not."

"What is wrong?"

'We are in trouble."

"And who are WE? Be specific Puppy."

"You, me, your world, my world."

"That is a big we."

"It is a big problem."

"Come on, Puppy. Don't be so mysterious. I am sure it can't be that bad."

"I was listening in at the last meeting the Dark Talents had with other psIs in the house. They are preparing for war."

'Oops, that sounds like a biggie. Are you sure?"

"I heard their plan. First they will intensify their efforts to find that Prophet, while they prepare for war. They want the Dark Talents to organize an army in my world and bring it over when needed. And your father agreed."

"My father would not agree to war."

"He did. He will organize the Dark Ones."

"That is terrible."

"It is."

"Will your people on your world agree?"

"Well, first of all, they don't have much choice. You know that the Dark Ones can force them to do anything. Besides, given the choice they would agree to this war."

"Puppy, you are hiding something. Remember, you are in a mind link."

"I know that."

"Then come clean. How do you know that your people will agree to come over to fight us?"

"Okay. I will tell you. You know that people on my world were not happy about how the Dark Ones were pushing us around."

"Yes. I remember. You told me about that."

"Well, for a long time now they have been planning to attack your world and stop you doing it."

"You told me that the barrier was closed to you."

'Yes. It is. I was sent here to find a way to cross it."

"Your people sent you here?"

"Yes."

"Why were you chosen for this?"

'My body shape is the closest to what you humans are able to accept."

"Why? Are the others all monsters?"

"To us, you are the monsters."

"So all that you told me about that bond between us and you wanting to come over was a lie?"

"No. It was all true. It just gave my people the chance to charge me with the mission."

"And were you successful?"

"In what?"

"Finding a way to cross the barrier."

'Yes and no..I did not find out anything new."

"You mean there is a way known to your people?"

"Yes, but it depends on the Dark Talents."

"Please explain."

"Well, if the Dark Ones bring over a large number of my people at the same time, the large breach of the barrier would weaken it enough for a lot of other people to come across."

"So what? The Dark Ones will control them."

"The Dark Talents con control only the ones they bring across. They won't even be aware of the other ones until it is too late."

"And this is exactly what would happen if there was a war"

"Correct. There will be a lot of dead people on all sides."

"All sides? How many sides will be in this war?"

The conflict will probably start between the two factions of the psIs. Your people and the Pacifists. When my people get involved, then the war will change to be in between your world and mine. Then the people you call stupis will get involved too."

"Are you sure all this will happen?"

"All I know is what your and my people are planning to do. I do not know what actually will happen."

....

It was a dark world, but surprisingly warm.

The air had an unpleasant, stingy smell, but was breathable.

Not a hint of green anywhere. Plants would not be able to survive in this perpetual half-darkness.

All around, both near and in the distance, tall mountain peaks threw flames and dark fumes into the air.

Dark figures moved, slithering on the ground, coming out from and disappearing intolarge , black holes.

There were black shapes moving everywhere, even in the air. In spite of the warmth of the air, Alice felt a chill running up and down her spine. She was happy for the comfort of the angor's silky body next to hers.

"So, this is your world?"

"Yes. Isn't she beautiful?"

"Well, beauty is in the eyes of the beholder, they say. At least now I know why you have such large eyes. I can hardly see anything."

"You will probably get used to the light."

"Is it always dark like this?"

"It is not really dark after you got used to it, but yes, it is always like this. We do not have days and nights as you do."

"How come? Isn't your planet turning?"

"Not around itself."

"Do you have any seasonal changes?"

"Not really. We go around our sun, but it is a dying red one, so except for some light it has not much of an influence on our world."

With all this volcanic activity all around, the origin of the heat and the smell was obvious, thought Alicia to herself .Holding on tight to the angor's fur

she was trying to slow down her heart.

Their arrival was so sudden and the view quite unexpected, frightening.

"Why are you so frightened?"

"You know, if a moviemaker wanted to make a really scary movie, this would be the perfect setting."

"Now you know how I feel on your world."

'I am also worried about how your people will react seeing a monster."

"What monster?"

"Me."

"Well, I am a bit worried about that too. Still, if the situation gets uncomfortable you can always disappear and go home. You know the way now."

"Tell me again why we are here? Your reasons were much more convincing when we talked about them at home."

"The idea was to convince my people that your world is not as bad as they think it is."

"It did sound logical at home, but now looking around I wonder if it was a good idea."

"I kind of agree. You look too alien here, even to me."

"That is not what I was thinking, but it is close enough."

"Do you want to go back?"

"No. If nothing else, I would like to see more of your world."

'Okay, let's go then."

"Go where?"

"I thought that first we could go to my home to see my parents."

"Your parents?"

'Yes, in this world I am a kid, just like you are on yours."

"I would have never pictured you as a little kid."

"Be quiet, we are nearly there."

"Where? I can see no homes anywhere."

"We live underground."

"In those holes?"

'In those underground homes."

There were moving shapes all around them now. Alice's watery eyes had trouble distinguishing the details of those multi limbed, bizarre appearances.

There were no sounds around them at all except for the odd footsteps and strange cricks and cracks.

They were walking along a kind of bumpy road, Alice still

holding on to the angor's fur, mostly for balance now as she
tripped a few times on the uneven ground.There were more and
more of the dark shapes around them,
following them on both sides of the road.
There still was not much sound around them, but the
threatening tension in the air was palpably increasing.
Those things were obviously very hostile towards her.
"We are nearly there."
They were approaching one of the larger holes along the
road.
There was a wide, long staircase leading down into the
semidarkness.
Alice had difficulty managing to walk down as the surface of
each step was inclined backwards and the edges were
irregularly rounded.
Still, she was happy about the length of the stairs as her eyes
had time to adjust to the low light.
There were a few very large, dark beings at the bottom of the
stairs, waiting for them.
By the shape of them, they were angors, but very large ones.
Nearly twice her angor's size.
"I can see now that you are a puppy, Puppy."
"Shut up."
A harsh mental command made them stop.
"Org, what have you brought here?"
"This is my friend Alice, my father. I was living at her home
until now."
"Kill that monster."
"She is my friend."
"Kill it or I will."
"You shouldn't and couldn't kill her. She is one of the
Controllers."

"And you bring it to my home?"

"I have been living with her family for a long time. I was treated with respect. I expected my family to do the same."

"You really want me to welcome a Controller into my home?"

"She is not just one of the Controllers. She is a very particular Controller. Her presence here could end the hostile situation between our worlds."

"I do not want to have any deals with a Controller."

"Father, please listen to her. The Controllers are planning to take a very large number of our people to form an army. There is a war about to start on their world and they need our help."

"Why would we help?"

"You know very well that you would have no choice in the matter with the Controllers."

"And you bring the enemy to my house?"

"She is not the enemy. She is trying to prevent the war on her world."

"What do I care if they kill each other? I rather welcome the idea."

"A lot of our people will die too."

"So it is here betraying its own people. Why should I trust it?"

"She is not betraying anyone. She is trying to prevent all those people dying on both sides."

"Okay Org. You know how much I hate the Controllers, but I trust your judgement. You would not have brought it here unless it was important, so I do not want to make a hasty decision.

Controller, you are not welcome in this house but you can stay for a while. I guarantee your safety at least until we work out what is happening.

I will call together a few leaders of our local community and you can present you case.

Org, I charge you to look after our uninvited guest. I suggest you stay in the house. You know how the people feel about Controllers, I cannot guarantee its safety if you go outside.

CHAPTER SIX

Carlos was growing up.

He was in high school now, with the big boys.

He adjusted well to the school situation and was accepted
well by his schoolmates.

Accepted, but still not very popular.

He was nice to everyone, so they liked him, but no one was
able to get close to him.

They tried, especially the girls.

He welcomed every approach but they never lasted long.

They could not get through the barrier of that strange
atmosphere that always surrounded him. They could not help
but feel the deep gap of difference which separated them from
the world he appeared to exist in. This strange, alien air that
surrounded him all the time, rejected any closer human
contact.

His teachers respected him because of his obvious
intelligence, but tried to avoid him as much as they could. It
was harder and harder to respond to his constant questioning
and quite embarrassing when they did not have the answers
for him.

His physics teacher just gave up; "Look Carlos, stop asking
me questions. You probably know more about physics than I
do. I should be asking the questions of you."

At home there were no significant changes.

Pietro accepted him as a weird puppy and let him do
whatever he wanted.

Maya was still his closest, his only friend.

They did everything together and the fact that she was
learning mind speech facilitated matters.

She was still very slow and sometimes aggravatingly so, but

the mental communication was always better than the vocal one. They didn't even had to be physically close to each other in order to talk.

This meant that they were still doing things together even when miles apart.

This also meant that Therezia was practically cut out of their everyday life.

She refused to learn mind speech.

She was able to accept as natural the things happening around her...natural to them. She wanted nothing to do with those activities.

The only real changes in Carlos's life were his teaching sessions with Magda and Steven.

They were vastly increased in intensity, not just at night, but many times during the day too, occupying practically every free minute in Carlos's life.

Carlos found very hard to cope with the demands of his teachers, but accepted it as he felt the increasing tension in Magda, the need to accomplish as much and as soon as it was possible.

Carlos felt that this push was a kind of preparation for fast approaching, threatening events and was doing all he could to follow Magda's instructions.

Magda also insisted that he keep up the contact with his friends, both at school and outside, although she did not give him much time to do so.

Carlos still managed to have some time to meet friends at the library, at someone's home or at the gym, which he really enjoyed.

Moya was there practically wherever he went.

They were accepted as a couple by everyone as they were rarely seen apart.

There was very little romance between them as Carlos's mind was not tuned in that direction, but when they were sitting or standing together somewhere, Moya was always very close at his side and both secretly enjoyed the accidental touch of arms or shoulders.

Maya was growing up too.

Although she still kept up the tomboyish behaviour, her style of dressing changed to a markedly girlish one.

Carlos appreciated this change when they were alone, but felt quite uncomfortable noticing the appreciative glances of the other boys.

....

"Magda, why can't I meet them?"

"Who?"

"The other kids."

"You meet a lot of kids every day."

"Kids that can do the same things than I do."

"No one can do the things you do."

"I mean the kids with an active mind. There are quite a lot of them around."

"How do you know that?"

"I am aware of them. I can feel their presence."

"Are they aware of you?"

"Of course not. You know that I close to the outside."

"Good. Keep it that way."

"You did not answer my question."

"What question was that?"

"Why can't I meet them?"

"Carlos, we have talked about this lots of times."

"No, we have not. You have never told me about the other kids."

"No, but we have talked about the importance of no one

becoming aware of you."

"Those kids are not going to harm me."

"Probably not, but they do not have the mental control you have. If they knew about you, everybody else would too."

"So what. You know quite well that I can protect myself."

"That is not the point."

"Then what is the point? I've really had enough of this secrecy that ties me down in all sort of ways and I have no idea why."

"I thought that you trusted me."

"I do, but isn't it time for you to trust me too?"

"It appears to be. Okay, let's talk about what I would rather not talk about as yet."

"Let's." "Carlos, how do you feel about the people whose mind is not open?"

"Like Pietro?"

'Yes, like him and a lot of others."

"I don't know. I have never thought about it. They are people, that's all."

'So why don't you show them what you can do?"

'Okay, I do understand that part. They are the majority, I would not fit. I would not have a place amongst them. They accept me now, I am part of the community because they do not know my real personality. What I do not understand is why would anybody want to harm me?"

"Carlos, I am really glad that you want to be part of human society, even if you have to hide your Talent. The problem is that not everyone thinks like you do."

"I did not think that anyone would want to be different."

"Well no, at least not the way you are thinking. What is happening is that within human society there is another, hidden society, very large and very active, formed by people with active minds."

"So, what is the problem?"

"The problem is that this PSI society is not united. It is divided into two factions and they do not like each other very much."

"I still can't see why anyone would want to harm me. I do not belong to any of the factions."

'Yes, you do. The factions are separated by their individual idea of how to relate to the non psi humans.

One group, called the Pacifists, wants to live peacefully with other humans, knowing that sooner or later the natural selection will make the whole world psi."

"Which is just logical thinking."

"Yes, and due to the way you think, you belong to this side. Still, there is another group, quite a large one too. People in this group are fed up with hiding and pretending, and do not want to wait many generations for the natural selection to change this. They want to come out into the open, now."

"How do they expect to achieve that?"

"By violence. By simple power, which they have, by overrunning and enslaving the human race."

"That is stupid."

"They have the power to do it."

"Okay, I see their point. Where do I come in?"

"You have powers no one else has. You could stop them. T hey are afraid of you."

"You can do lots more things than I can do."

"Steven and I have similar Talents to yours, but far less power."

"Then how come...?"

"When you have lived as long as I have, you will be much stronger than I am now."

"I still can't see why I am in danger? I would not do anything to anyone."

"There is a kind of legend amongst our people. That one day, a Prophet with great power will arrive and unite our people with humanity."

"Every minority group, throughout history has a similar legend.That a hero will come and save them. It is stupid to believe in legends today."

"That is a logical statement, but people are not logical. People are basically emotional, and there, the legend fits perfectly."

"And they think I am that Prophet?"

"I do not think that the leaders believe that but your existence has such propaganda value that they cannot afford to have you on the opposite side."

"And because they do not expect to be able to convert me to their side, they have to eliminate me."

"Exactly my point. So now you understand why I am trying to protect you."

"Then what is next? What do we do, now that I know about this?"

"Nothing changes. That is why I waited with the explanation. This is a distracting thought and you do not need distractions now."

"So this is why you are pushing me so hard to practice?"

"Yes. You have to develop your Talent as far as possible before you come out into the open. Sooner or later you will have to face them and it will not be a friendly encounter."

,,,,,,,,,,,,,,,,,,,,,,,,,,,

Magda was right about what she said about distraction.

The whole thing was going around and around in Carlos's mind. It is not easy to ignore the fact that out there, there is large group of people who want to kill you.

Carlos was clear about his capacities and felt that he could defend himself against anyone, human or animal.

But those psis were another thing.

He never met anyone, apart from his teachers, with psi capacities and had no idea what they were able to do.

He practiced putting himself in situations of danger and always believed himself safe.

But these psis, they were an unknown factor. He had to learn more about them to be able to plan his defence.

He practiced extending his awareness further and further around him, picking up life signatures of living things in the neighbourhood.

He was very familiar with these signatures; he had felt them many times during the years.

But as he was extending his awareness further out, he started to pick up life signatures that were unusually bright and strong, they stood far out from the others.

He realized that these signatures were from psi people.

As he never had tried before, Carlos was really surprised how far he could extend his awareness. He was able to perceive the presence of psi entities from quite a distance.

There were quite a few of them around.

There was also a very large concentration of those very bright mental sparks in one location, and the surprising thing for Carlos was that at that particular spot, he could find no normal human presence.

That spot was a private school just a few blocks away from where he lived.

"So they also have their own school. A school just for psi kids and psi teachers. They must be very well organized."

So much psi presence in the neighbourhood at first worried Carlos, but he scanned those minds and could not find any of them strong enough to be able to penetrate his mental barrier and detect his presence.

Feeling safe, one day he decided to stand across the street from the school, watching them file out at the end of the school day, to go home.

All of them had a very active mind but no one appeared to give him much attention.

However, there were a few amongst them who looked at him strangely, but no one made a comment.

Carlos realized that to people who were used to seeing life signatures, he would appear strangely blank behind his barrier. From then on he avoided going close to the school or to any of the bright mental signatures, realizing that his presence could be detected by his lack of mental identification.

Still, he wanted to know more about them so he scanned their minds from a distance, always careful not to be noticed by them.

Carlos was really surprised with the large variety of Talents those active minds had.

The diversity of the extra capacities was impressive, but in spite of that Carlos did not find anything which could represent a threat to him. He realized that he was scanning only young, undeveloped minds, and that the adults would be more powerful, still, even taking that into account, he did not feel any reason to worry.

There were, however, a couple of minds he didn't really understand.

Only a very few of them, but the quality of their mind structure puzzled Carlos. They were strange minds, unusually structured with a rare, twisted quality.

They were obviously psi minds, very active, very intelligent, but the Talents of those minds was...well, Carlos just could not work it out.

Magda naturally knew about them when Carlos questioned her.

"They are the Dark Ones. Better stay clear of them."

"Why? Are they dangerous?"

"Yes, but not in an obvious way. They have a strange Talent which does not belong to this world."

"What can they do?"

"Well, they do not have much power in this world, but they have a Talent that enables them to call entities from outside to do their bidding."

"Outside? From where outside?"

"From a parallel dimension. Have you heard about them?"

"A bit. They are worlds that physically occupy the same space as ours, but at another energy level, completely separated from ours."

"Yes, that is it. The Dark Ones have the capacity to bring over living things from there."

"People?"

"I am not sure you can call them people. The majority have strange body shapes."

"What kind of shapes?"

"The few ones I know about look like demons or gargoyles but probably there are lot of other shapes too."

"And they come over willingly?"

'Not quite. They do not really have choice in the matter."

"Are they dangerous?"

"Not to you. They have mainly physical aptitudes and any physical power is no match to your mind control."

There was one other thing Carlos encountered with his distant mind scanning.

Something he did not like at all. It was the general attitude, a complete disregard and lack of respect towards the non psi humans.

They called them stupis and ignored them completely, considered them lower than animals.

"What kind of people teach children to feel like that? This is very wrong."-Carlos commented to Magda.

"Now you understand why it would be so easy for them to get rid of the non psi humans. If the war starts, those humans have no chance of surviving."

....

Moya was getting frustrated with her training with Magda. She worked really hard, like always when she wanted to achieve something, but this one was very difficult for her.

She was able to receive thought messages now from Magda and Carlos, providing they sent them with large intensity, but had problems with sending out her own thoughts.

She managed to send out a few words or concepts with a lot of concentration, but was far away from being able to have a mental conversation.

Magda kept encouraging her to continue practicing, but even she admitted that the training had started a bit late. Moya's mind was already set in its way on the physical world and it was hard to remodel it for mental activities.

Magda really started to respect her seeing the effort she was putting into the practicing.

"The willpower Moya has, is unusual for a person her age." Moya was also changing in many different ways.

Her appearance now was definitely that of a girl, and a very pretty one at that.

Part of her boyish behaviour remained; she still enjoyed a game of soccer and beating the neighbourhood's boys at it, or going fishing with Carlos, but lately that was not quite enough for her.

She was restless, irritated. Something was missing from her life and she really did not know what it was.

And Carlos was not a big help.

They still spent a lot of time together and enjoyed each other's company, but Moya wished Carlos would be just a little bit more sensitive.

That he would notice how good it felt to be close to each other, just standing there, nearly touching.....

Terezia was watching them with a smile on her face.

She really liked Moya and was happy with the bond which so obviously was growing in between the two of them.

Wherever they went they were accepted as a couple, even at their age, the attraction was so noticeable to everyone. To everyone but themselves.

....

"So why are you telling me this now?"

"What do you mean why I am telling you this? You are the Chief of Police and my daughter is missing. Who the hell should I be telling?"

"That was not what I meant and you know it. Your daughter went missing over a week ago. Why are you telling me about it just now?"

"Because I thought I knew where she went and that I would be able to get her back."

"And you were wrong."

"Obviously. Well, not quite, I still think I know where she is. Just failed to find her."

"And where do you think she is?"

"Well, it is a little complicated."

"That does not help me much."

"Okay. You know about our Talent, that we are able to contact living entities not belonging to our world."

"I know a bit about it. A parallel universe."

"That is the theory but we do not really know for sure. We just bring them over, and then send them back, not really knowing where they come from."

"Didn't you ever try to find out?"

"There were a few half-hearted attempts but they all failed. Seeing the beings that came over no one really wanted to go there."

"So in reality you just reach out in the dark and grab whatever is there."

"It is nearly like that. Like when you go out fishing on your boat, you throw your hook into the water, you do not exactly know where it goes, and you catch the fish that just happens to be there."

"And what does this have to do with your daughter's disappearance?"

"I believe that she went to that world."

"You mean that your little girl achieved something that all you Dark Ones have failed to do over the years ?"

"She is not that little and she is very smart for her age. And yes, that is what I think."

"Why do you think...?"

"She had a pet dog, a very large one, which came from that other world. They both disappeared."

"So what? They both could be anywhere."

"Not quite. That dog would call attention to it wherever they would be."

"Okay. The next question. If you believe that she is there, what do you want me to do? I do not have your Talent. I cannot search for her there."

"I believe that she is there but I have no way to be sure. I am currently organizing my people to carry out a very large search on that world but I would like to cover all possibilities. That is where you come in."

"I can see your point and I agree with you. The problem is, that if we assume that they are in this world, well, after all this time, they could be anywhere. I will have to organize a nationwide search, probably wider."

"Do you have the personnel for that?"

"Not really. I will have to involve the regular police force."

"You mean the stupis?"

"They are not that bad. They are well organized and will be able to do very thorough search."

"What are you going to tell them?"

"Just the truth. A missing girl, a worried father, the usual things. Of course you will have to be ready to answer some questions."

"But we keep everything on this world?"

"Of course. You cover your world and I will do everything I can on this one."

....

Carlos had a bad day.

From the moment he woke up in the morning he had this feeling that something was about to happen.

He was not sure what it was, did not even know if it would be a good thing or a bad one, but was certain that it would be something important.

Something which would change his life in a significant way.

Carlos did not have the Talent to foresee future events, still, he had in the past become aware of things that had not happened as yet.

But just in a hazy, nonspecific way.

Not enough to know what would actually happen, but enough to make him worry about the prospect.

Magda explained to him that even if he did not have a specific Talent, a well-trained psi mind was open to a large variety of influences.

So, he was worried now, not knowing what to expect.

He did not like this feeling of being a sitting duck, just waiting for something to happen.

The morning went by uneventfully.

He went to school, no issues there.

During all day at school, still a criminally wasted time in his opinion, nothing unexpected happened.

Carlos was sitting at his desk, paying very little attention to his teachers, scanning the minds around him as far as he could reach.

Nothing, and nothing again.

Still, this approaching feeling was getting stronger as the day went on.

A very uncomfortable feeling.

School finished, with nothing untoward happening.

While leaving school amongst a large number of schoolmates, Carlos had this sudden realization that it was time.

Whatever it was what was going to happen, was going to happen now!

He spread his mind scanning the environment around him and became aware of people concentrating their attention on his person.

On the other side of the street, just across the school, there was a young boy with a little girl, standing side by side, looking at him with intense concentration.

Their mind was guarded, but they were very obviously psi minds.

The little girl was signalling him with her hands, indicating that she wanted him to cross the street to meet them.

The tension disappeared from Carlos's mind.

So this was the expected, important happening.

It did not appear to be too bad.

A superficial scan did not reveal anything threatening.

Carlos knew that he could force their mental barriers to find out what they were about, but not without them being aware of it. They were psis after all.

He decided not to force things and crossed the street to meet them.

"Do I know you?"

The little girl was taking up the conversation. The boy was just observing, with the quiet intensity of a psi.

"We have never met before but we two have spent a lot of time trying to find you."

"Why would you want to find me? And before you answer that, how did you find me? I thought that my mental barrier was closed to outside search."

"You kind of miscalculated there. Your barrier is absolutely perfect, but that was exactly what allowed us to find you. To a telepath you are standing far out in the middle of a crowd. You have the only mind around here that is completely closed, so you stand out."

"I didn't think about that. I will be more careful in the future."

"You are lucky that we were the first to find you."

"First? That is your cue to explain why you were looking for me."

"Could we go somewhere else? I feel uncomfortable having a conversation in the middle of the street."

"There is a park just around the corner."

The park was a really nice one.

Large trees for shade, wide benches all over, with a little lake right in the middle.

There were even a few white ducks in the water.
Terezia had insisted once when they were here, that they
were young swans but Carlos knew that they were ducks.
The three preferred to sit on the grass facing each other.
"Well...."-Carlos was getting impatient.
"Okay. First let us clarify who we are. You know about the two
factions our people are divided into. I believe you belong to
the group called Pacifists. I am Angelina and he is Peter,
and we belong to the Activists group."
'You two are the first people I've met from that group."
"And it is lucky for you, as the Activist leaders would not be
very friendly."
'I was told about that. What about you two?"
"I can assure you that we've come with a white flag, very
friendly in fact. The truth is that we need your help to avoid
something dreadful happening in the very near future. And
when I say we, I do not mean only us two, or only our side of
things."
"I am very interested in what you have to say, but would it be
okay if I call my teacher to be present? She is a very wise
woman and I take her advice very seriously."
"That would be fine. Actually, I've been dying to meet Magda
for a very long time."
"You seem to know a lot about me. Anyhow, here she is."
At that very moment, a dark shadow condensed next to the
nearest tree.
With a few steps, the tall, woman dressed all in black, was
standing next to them.
"Wow. I did not know anyone could do that."
"She is not just anyone."
"I know. She is a legend amongst us. Very nice to meet you at
last Magda."

"Thank you children, it is very nice to meet you too, although I cannot say that I am happy about the fact that everybody knows about me."

"I didn't quite say that. What I meant was that you are a legend amongst any group of psi people, but at the same time I do not believe that anyone actually knows much about you.""Thank you. That sounds much better. I think you two have got something to tell Carlos."

"Well, in a nutshell. You know about the Activists' intention to come out into the open and declare their rights. Recently the decision was made and an open war is imminent."

"That is a very serious statement. I was not aware of this, although I knew that something was brewing."

"That is only the half of it!"

"I hope the other half is not as bad."

"It is worse. The Dark Ones are involved, and they are organizing to bring an army from the other world for the war."

"This is very bad. What I can't see is why you two are telling us all this. You know that we must try to stop them.""No one can stop them. They've planned this for years and they are very strong. A lot of innocent people will die. Only one person, the Prophet has the chance to prevent the war and all the killing."

"And who is that Prophet?"

"Carlos."

"Who? Me?"

"Yes, you Carlos. I don't know what is that you can do about the situation, but no one else has a chance."

"What I still don't know is what you two are doing here?"

"Our parents have been working very hard to find you and eliminate you from the opposition. You disappeared so perfectly that no one was able to pinpoint your location. By pure luck Angelina found a way to follow the effects of your barrier. Fortunately, and by pure chance, no one else has thought of doing that so far."

'So, what are your plans now? You two have embarked on a quest very few would dare to even consider."

"We don't have a plan. We were only trying to find you and ask for your help. There is only the two of us, no one else knows about this meeting. As you, Carlos appear to be one of the main characters in this show, even if you do not know it, we expected you to be able to do something.

I don't like the idea of so many people dying. Perhaps you could meet with our leaders and come to a friendly arrangement."

Carlos was not sure what he was expected to say and was looking to Magda for advice.

She was quiet for a while, with her eyes closed, and appeared to be in deep concentration, but she was not just thinking. She was scanning the surroundings for unwanted attention directed towards them, then scanned the children's mind without them being aware of her. Before making a decision she wanted to make sure that she knew everything about what they were talking about.

Then with a deep sigh she looked at their visitors.

"Children, I am sure that everything you have said was the truth and I also know that you came here with the best of intentions. You came here trying to prevent a very nasty war, but what you have actually achieved, was to precipitate it."

"You can't mean that."

"Sadly, I do. The moment your parents become aware of where you went and what you told us, they will have no choice but to immediately do two things.

One is to declare war, even if they are not quite ready for it.

They cannot afford to give us time to prepare.

The other is to attack Carlos, because, as you have said, they can't have him on the opposite side, and now they will know where to find him."

"We will not say anything about this meeting to anyone."

'I know. That is your intention. Still, the moment you get home your parents will be aware of what happened, in every detail. Your barriers are just not strong enough to hide it from them."

"So what can we do? We did not want to put you in danger or to start a war."

"It is your choice but you know what will happen if you go home now."

"What else can we do? Where else could we go?"

"If you so decide, you are welcome to stay at my home for a while. I know that it is not a nice thing to do to your parents, but you know the alternative.""For how long would we have to stay?"

"Not too long. Until we make some sort of plan about how we should deal with this situation."

....

"Hi Ronald, and how is the Chief of Police?"

"Hi. The Chief of Police is fine, thank you. And how is the leader of the Dark Ones?"

"I am fine too. I am calling you to find out what is going on."

"I was just about to phone you for the very same reason."

"Good. That would mean that you have found my girl."

"Not quite. Actually I've got nothing to tell you about that. I have a huge number of people out there looking for her, but so far, absolutely nothing. I am beginning to believe that you were right the first time."

"I was right about what?"

"When you said that she might be on that other world, because on this one we could not find any trace of her. What is happening on your side of things?"

"The same thing. No trace of her. However, our search is very limited as we cannot go there to look around. We can get the natives to come here but communication is very limited. Our chance of finding her there is close to nil."

"I don't know what to tell you except that we have to keep trying."

"Thank you. I am relying on you."

"There is another thing that may or may not be related to your daughter's disappearance.

Two other of our leaders reported their children missing."

"That can hardly be a coincidence."

"Exactly my thoughts. Someone appears to be collecting our leader's children, but why?"

"Someone is trying to establish leverage in order to manipulate us."

"That did cross my mind but only the Pacifists would benefit from such a thing."

"This is not their style."

"Correct. Then who and why?"

"I've got a deep connection with Alicia. I f my daughter was hurt, I would know about it. So far, though, I think she is fine, wherever she is."

'That is the same as what the other parents said. So if they are well, where are they?"

"Then this is really up to you. I would not look for the other children in the parallel world."

"It could also be just a prank the children are playing."

"Alicia would not do that."

"Then what do you suggest we should do? What we have

been doing so far does not seem to be working."

"I think it is time to contact Magda's group."

"If you are going to accuse her with stealing our children she would get upset. And you do not want Magda to be upset."

"No. I would not do that. I was only thinking of asking for her help in locating the children."

"Well, if anyone can do it, it would be her. Go ahead with it."

....

The house was as unusual as you would expect Magda's home to be.

Although it was built on a large corner block, due to its dark colours and perhaps its unkempt appearance, it looked quite small from the outside.

The large, green trees practically hid the top part of the building and the weeds that overgrew the garden covered everything on the ground.

But when you crossed the very heavy wooden door, and entered the house, it was quite different.

Inside it was very large, wide open with large windows that filled the house with light.

Sparsely furnished with old fashioned but very comfortable furniture.

Practically all the walls, from floor to ceiling, were covered with bookshelves heavy with books of all sorts.

There were very few ornaments around, some small statues of unusual shapes and a few old looking photographs. The whole house was organized to be functional and comfortable. It was very clean, not a speck of dust anywhere. Even the books, though some of them quite old, were clean and dust free.

In every corner of every room, on the bookshelves, on the windowsills, in fact everywhere in the house, there were large, purple crystals of different shapes catching the sunlight streaming in.

Even in the garden, partly covered by weed, one could catch those purple flashes all over the place.

They were Magda's eyes and ears, through these she could expand her mind and be fully aware of her surroundings.

All together it was a nice house, but not designed for children. Magda and the children were sitting at the wide dining room table in deep conversation.

This meaning that Peter and Angelina were discussing the day's events, while Magda, across the table, was watching them with a small smile on her face. On close observation one would see the lines of concentration on her forehead, eyes focused on nothing, deep in thought.

After a while, even the children noticed that Magda was not with them anymore and left her alone. They had enough to talk about.

Although they understood Magda's reasoning in keeping them with her, they were quite worried about what was happening at home as a result of their not returning.

They could not notify their parents and no one knew where they were. Their parents were probably worried sick. This was the second day they were missing and they had no idea when they could go home.

Every now and then they glanced at Magda, as though expecting her to say something.

Anything.

They started to be really frightened about not knowing what would happen to them now, and about what will happen when they eventually got home.

How to explain things to their parents?

They began to regret going on their quest to find the Prophet without really thinking through the possible consequences. Why couldn't they have left things alone and let the adults take care of everything

The slowly growing fear inside them started to cloud their logical thinking, to make them doubt the original reasons for starting all of this.

They were psi children, but they were children after all and had their limitations.

If at least Magda would give them some explanation, if she would just give them some idea about what was going on in her mysterious mind, it might help a little.

As on cue, Magda straightened in her chair and was looking at them with more colour on her cheeks.

"Children, we have some unexpected visitors."

At the same time the door chime went off quite loudly, indicating someone at the door.

"The door is open, come in Steven."-Magda called out in a raspy voice.

Steven walked in with a "Thank you Magda." –hand in hand with a little girl, leaving the door wide open behind him, as if expecting someone else to follow.

"I have with me a young person here who wanted to see you Magda. She put out a very widely open mental call trying to contact you. I blocked the call and thought it better to bring her to you before she called too much attention all around."

"You have done the right thing, thank you Steven. Please come in Alicia. I have here some friends of yours who I am sure would be glad to see you.

Who is that strange mind outside? Why doesn't he want to come in, Steven?"

"He is Alicia's companion. He would prefer to stay outside

until Alicia explains the situation to you."

"Steven, please tell him that I have met people from his world before, that he can come inside in peace, and sit down in a corner until he is ready to talk to us."

A dark form appeared in the door.

A very tall, slim figure, covered from head to toe in a black, hooded cape.

Except for the very big, bright eyes his face was hidden by the hood, just as his whole body was by the long cape that reached down to the floor. Even his hands were covered by the wide sleeves of the cape.

With a very slight nod of his head the figure retired to the most distant corner of the room and sat down on a small chair there.

The children were really surprised as this was the last place they expected to see each other.

They hugged, jumping and shouting, crying and laughing all at the same time.

All three had a lot on their minds, and this unexpected meeting of close friends brought them great relief to their worries.

"Okay children, let's sit down at the table. You all have a lot of things to talk about but first I would like Alicia to explain her presence in my house."

They were all psi children, they all knew discipline.

It was Alicia turn to talk. She started very unsure of herself.

"Please forgive my intrusion to your house. I did not know what else to do. I expected to be of help to a lot of people but what I got myself into at the end is just too much for me to handle.

I am not even sure that I have done the right thing coming here.

I have heard a lot about you and thought that you would be the ideal person to tell me what to do. Now I am not so sure. When Steven picked up my search call he promised to bring me here to see you. I thought that all of my problems would be solved.

I am not even sure how to begin to tell you about the things I wanted to achieve."

"Alicia, let me make it easier for you. I know about the imminent war between the psi fractions and I also know about the Dark Ones organizing an army from the other world. I also know that you have disappeared from home and your parents are very worried, looking for you everywhere.

Now, please tell me where you have been and what you achieved there. It had to be a great deal if you were able to bring back with you that person sitting in the corner.

I have also noticed that he is here on his own will and not under your control, which is very unusual to say the least. I have never heard of this happening before."

"Well, it is a rather long story. Do you know about Puppy, my dog?"

"I have heard about him."

"We judged him first by his shape and took him for a dog. He turned out to be a rather intelligent young person who taught me mind speech and how to travel to his world, which is open to me now.

After a lot of trouble, as the people there were openly hostile towards me for being one of what they call "Controllers", eventually their leaders got together and listened to my story. They took it all very seriously. In spite of their frightening appearance, they are a very peaceful race and would prefer to avoid the violence and the loss of life a war would mean. They sent back one of their leaders with me. He has authority to make decisions and wants to negotiate with our leaders. My problem now is how to get them together, This is where I hope you can help me."

"Wow! Alicia, from now on I will never again call you a child. What you have achieved here required so much guts and smart thinking that I know very few adults able to do something similar. I really admire you.

All three of you achieved things our whole psi society failed to do. I am sure your parents will be very proud of you when you eventually get home.

Now let's talk about this person you brought with you. What is his name? What should I call him?"

"He answers to the name Zor.dox.gohn and because of his facial shape he has difficulty with vocalization but he is very good at mind speech. In his world he is a powerful, very respected person."

"No problem. Zor.dox.gohn, would you please sit with us so we can talk to each other?" The tall figure stood up with a slight nod of his head and approached the table. They could not see how he walked as even his feet were covered by that cape thing, but he did not make any noise while approaching. Not a sound.

In the same way he sat down on a chair across the table from them.

"How do you want me to address you, black lady?"

"You can call me Magda, and I would appreciate if you could remove your hood. I feel very uncomfortable talking to someone when I cannot see his face."

"In my world, my race never shows their faces. It is a custom we are serious about. I am sorry for your discomfort."

"It is a strange custom to us, but I can accept it .Tell me Zor.dox.gohn- what made you come to our world?"

"This little person approached us with a terrible story. She willingly opened her mind for us to scan so we could see the veracity of her tale.

We took her message very seriously.

The problem is that due to her age and social position her knowledge is very limited. So I followed her across to learn more, and mainly, to try to avoid the predicted catastrophe. She believed that you could put me in contact with the decision makers of this world."

"I think I will be able to do just that, but it will need a lot of planning.

First we will have to get together with the leaders of the two opposing parties preparing the war, which will be no easy task.

Then we will have to introduce you to them, which will be harder still, as you represent the third side of this war.

In the meanwhile please accept the hospitality of my house and give us time to plan and arrange things."

....

The table was very large, made of a beautiful dark reddish wood, the legs finely carved and the top inlaid with dark figures which seemed to dance in the flickering light of the room.

There were twenty men sitting around its long, oval shape, all very solemn, and elegantly dressed.

There was a low murmur of conversation along the table, all waiting for the meeting to begin.

The Chief of Police stood up from his chair at the end of the table.

"Thank you all for responding so quickly to my call and please accept my sincere apologies for the inconvenience this might have caused you.

I have brought forward our monthly meeting as we have a few rather urgent problems to discuss.

Most of you already know about these problems, so I'll get straight to the point. The first thing I would like to discuss is the mysterious disappearance of our children.

Normally I would not bring cases of missing children to this meeting but when three of our leaders, one by one, reported their children missing, I considered this very suspicious.

I have to consider the possibility of this being the beginning of some sort of hostility against our people.

Especially as the three parents targeted are the main protagonists in our plans for the future."

There was a consenting murmur along the table.

"During the last ten days I have organized a large part of the local and intestate police force to find the children and I am sorry to report that all our efforts have so far failed. We simply have arrived at the point where it would appear that there is nothing else we can do."

"What about the children? You can't just stop there."

"Of course we will not give up, although everything seems to be pointless. So I decided to call for help from outside the police force. I have called Magda to help us."

There was a sudden silence in the room, but it did not last long.

It was followed soon by indignant exclamations and angry comments from all around the table.

"Why Magda? She is not exactly on our side."

"The Pacifists are the only ones who would benefit from all of this and here you are, calling their leader for help?"

"Magda has never done anything for us."

"I do not trust Magda. Quite possibly it was her who took the children."

The Chief of Police waited for a while with a deep frown on his
face. The angry comments did not seem to stop. Eventually
he had enough.He slammed both palms on the table in front of
him and
raised his voice.

"Quiet!....You have elected me as the leader of this council
and to make decisions in your name.
So I have made a decision which I felt it was proper in this
situation. I called on Magda for help. She will be here very
soon. The main reason I have called you here was so all of
you could witness this meeting."

"But why Magda? It was probably she, who took the children."

"Magda assured me that she had nothing to do with the
disappearance of the children."

"What did you expect her to say?"

"Magda could be on the opposite side but I still trust her.
Kidnapping children is not her way of doing things.""Thanks you
for the vote of confidence, Chief."

The deep female voice startled everyone. A quiet voice but
one which seemed to fill the room with a strange resonance.

"Magda! What are you doing here?"

"I had the impression that I was invited."

"You were. Sorry. Your sudden appearance confused me. I
was expecting at least a knock on the door."

"I did not use the door."

"I gathered that much. The door is locked and two people are
there to guard it."

"Do you want me to leave?"

"No, of course not. I do apologize for my brusque reaction, but
you surprised me. Please
sit down. One of you gentlemen please bring the lady a chair."

"Do not bother for me, Could I use that side table there

Chief?"

"Yes, Of course, but..."

The small table next to the wall started to move across the room towards the dark figure. On the way it appeared to melt, to lose its form, then to solidify again into a new shape. By the time it got next to the woman it was a very comfortable-looking chair.

"That was quite impressive Magda."

"I will change it back to its original shape before I leave. So, what is it that you wanted to talk to me about, so urgently?"

"Well, you know about my problem. You said you could help me."

'Yes. The children. You do not have to worry about them. They are very well, all three of them."

"You know where they are?"

"Yes. At my house."

"At your...What are they doing there!."

"When I left them to come here they were working out the mathematical relationship between the length of the tail on my cat and the possible speed it could run at."

"Does this mean that you...?"

"No. It was not me. The children presented themselves at my house of their own will, quite unexpectedly, without me doing anything about it."

"Why would they go to your house?"

"They were in the same situation that you are in. They had problems they felt only I could help them with."

"What kind of problems?"

"Chief, if you really want to know what is happening, I would suggest you stop asking questions and let me tell you the story without interruption.

I am glad that you called together these gentlemen as all of you should hear what I am about to tell you. I am afraid that some of your plans for the future will have to change."

"Please go ahead. I will not interrupt you."

"Thank you. Let me talk first about Peter and Angelina. Alicia has a story of her own. All three of them are very intelligent children, demonstrating capacities far beyond their age. Their parents should be proud of them.

Okay. Let us begin with Peter and Angelina. These two children were aware of your hostile activities and were very upset about the innocent victims being involved. Yes, I know about you planning a war. As a matter of fact, I have known about it before the children mentioned it. Anyway, back to Peter and Angelina. They felt, being children, that it was their duty to try and do something in order to ease what they expected the result of this war to be.

They had heard a lot of rumours about a Prophet, who, based on the capacities these rumours gave him, would be able to assist.

So they decided to find this Prophet and ask him for advice. They actually achieved this, they talked to the Prophet, who contacted me, and eventually I had the honour of them being guests in my house."

"How did they find the Prophet?"

"I expected that question, as I am aware that your people have been trying, and failing to find him for a long time. These children were very smart. They began with the same assumption that you all have, that the Prophet has a very powerful mental arsenal and they concluded that to protect himself he had to have also a very strong mental barrier to close his thoughts from prying minds.

They also knew that everyone has some degree of mental leakage which a telepath could perceive. So they looked for the person with perfect mental silence and found the Prophet."

"Very ingenious, but still does not explain their presence at your house."

"As I have said, they are very smart, They realized that the moment they got home you would know about the Prophet which in turn would put his life in danger. They also realized that by what they had told me about your plans, you would be forced to attack immediately, and hence precipitating the very war they were trying to prevent."

"So?"

"So they decided not to go home until some kind of solution was found."

"And was this solution found?"

"Yes. After this conversation you will change your plan for the future."

"Those are very strong words even from you Magda, but please continue with your explanation."

"Okay. Let me talk about Alicia now, as she has a very important part in this story.

You all know about her pet dog. That being from another world. Due to its exterior appearance, it was taken to be a common dog. As such, it was free to move around the house. Its presence was ignored, even at the highly secretive meetings which were taking place in the house. It was only a dog, after all.

As it happens, in spite of its body shape, that being was a very intelligent, sentient person, who was sent by his people to spy on humans, especially the Dark Ones, to find a way to stop the human intrusion in their life.

This dog shaped person explained the situation to Alicia. She was chosen for this because she was the only person around with an open mind and willing to listen.

He told Alicia that while listening at your meetings he heard your plans about organizing a large army on his world and then bringing it over here to help your cause. What you did not know was that by bringing over a large number of persons, you would weaken the barrier, allowing them to cross over by themselves. This would mean a very large and very hostile alien army arriving to our world.

And the majority of these, would not be under your control, you wouldn't even be aware of them.

The end result would be a war between two worlds, with a very large number of casualties on both sides.

So the alien thing asked the only human who was in a position to listen, that is, Alicia, for help in avoiding the catastrophe."

"Why Alicia?"

'She was the only person he was able to communicate with."

"So, once again. How did she finish at your house?"

"Now, that is a very interesting story. Alicia decided to do something I do not think any adult person would dare to do. She decided to go to that parallel world to sort things out."

"How the hell did she do that? We have all tried to do so, on numerous occasions, and failed. "- exploded the leader of the Dark Ones

'Well, leader of the Dark Ones, she not only managed to do so, but now that world is permanently open to her. But let me finish the story. I am at the end of it now. Alicia had a lot of problems in that world as she was considered to be part of the invading humans, and people were openly hostile to her to the point that her life was in danger quite often. Fortunately, she managed eventually to make them listen to her story and she returned with one of their leaders to clarify their relationship with humans."

"Still, that does not explain..."

"Her presence in my house. I know, but the explanation is
very simple. That ambassador wants to meet with human
leaders. She could not arrange that.
She could not bring him home to you either due to your
attitude towards beings from that world. He is here free, by his
own will and would not stay free for long amongst the Dark
Ones.
I appeared to her to be the only solution."

"So when are the children coming home?"

"The moment we come to a common agreement."

"You mean you and me?"

"Yes. Let me make a conclusion to the story. The end result is
that the alien army prepared by the Dark Ones is out of the
picture.
You cannot bring them over to our world.
Without them you have not enough strength to carry out your
hostile plans.
You also know that the Pacifist group has the more powerful
minds. If you try to attack us in any way you would lose.
I will leave you now, to allow you to freely discuss things
amongst yourselves and to make a decision. I will return in
about one hour, with the children, with the Prophet and the
ambassador from that world.
You can let me know then about your decision."

The black clad tall figure slowly faded out until it completely
disappeared. In the same instant, the small table was back
against to the wall.

....

Later on, they didn't even thank her for retuning the children.

Milton Keynes UK
Ingram Content Group UK Ltd.
UKHW011116281123
433341UK00022B/236